The Saxon Princess

LADIES OF VALOR SERIES

ANNE R BAILEY

INKBLOT PRESS

This one is for Oliver, my loyal companion, you will be missed.

Also by Anne R Bailey

Ladies of the Golden Age

Countess of Intrigue

The Pirate Lord's Wife

The Lady of Fortune

The Lady's Season (Novella)

Ladies of Valour

The Saxon Princess

The Queen's Fight (Coming soon)

Royal Court Series

The Lady Carey

The Lady's Crown

The Lady's Ambition

The Lady's Gamble

The Lady's Defiance

The Lady Ursula

Forgotten Women of History

Joan

Fortuna's Queen

Thyra

Bluehaven Series

The Widowed Bride

Choosing Him

Other

The Stars Above

You can also follow the author at: www.inkblotpressco.ca

PART ONE
1093

ONE

Edith sat beside her mother, eyes demurely fixed on her lap like a dutiful daughter. Some might have mistaken her for praying as the doctors murmured among themselves. She was not praying; she was gritting her teeth to keep from shouting. Her hands were not clasped together in devotion but rather frustration.

Her mother was ill and no one had found a cure.

Yet.

But they would. Edith was sure of it.

In the meantime, her mother—her pious mother—refused to keep to her bed.

"Your Grace," one of the doctors said, stepping forward with a deep bow. "It is our professional opinion that your humors are out of balance. A prolonged rest and the application of leeches would be most beneficial, along with a diet of meat to strengthen you."

"I am fasting."

"Your confessor told us." The doctor bowed his capped

3

head. "He also assured us that he could get you a dispensation. As you know, the church allows for exceptions —"

"I believe that the state of my soul is not under your jurisdiction."

From her vantage point, Edith could see how the doctor's lips thinned, ready to argue. "Your Grace—" he began, then, thinking better of it, said, "I apologize. Of course you are correct." For a brief moment his gaze flicked to Edith, almost as if he wished she would say something.

Even if she dared, it wouldn't make a difference.

Only her father had the authority to command her, the Queen of Scotland, to obey the wishes of her doctors. But on the eve of battle he was distracted. At this very moment, he was somewhere in the castle, making plans with his generals, studying his maps, or sharpening his sword. Edith would give anything to have him here.

"Then we shall go prepare a draught to help bring harmony to your humors. When you feel it is time, we hope you will allow us to treat you further with leeches and cupping. In the meantime, allowing yourself to rest is of the utmost importance to your well-being."

"Thank you, I will keep that in mind," her mother said.

The doctor bowed and Edith watched her mother dismiss him with an imperious wave of her hand.

Once the team of physicians had left the room, her mother wasted no time and ordered her maids to help her get ready and pull out her best gown.

As they rushed to fetch everything she would need from her chests and the pegs on the wall, Margaret turned to Edith.

"And you, my daughter, shall help me with my hair."

Edith hesitated. The tremor in her mother's hand as she held out the comb revealed how much she was straining to remain upright in her seat. She wondered if there was some way to get her mother to return to her bed instead.

"Edith."

The warning reproach in her mother's voice was enough to make the thirteen-year-old girl jump into action. The white linen cap was removed, and Edith set about unraveling the heavy braids. It was a pity her mother's golden hair had faded and become streaked with white. Yet as Edith worked the comb through and applied rosehip oil into the hair, it began to shine and fall into soft waves down her back. Today her mother wouldn't hide her hair behind a veil but wear it loose with a simple circlet of gold as adornment.

"Will Father really ride out?" Edith asked in a low whisper.

She heard her mother's soft sigh. "He will. The insult to him has been great. He will make a show of force, and we, his womenfolk, must support him."

Edith considered her mother's words. *Must.* A wife had to show utter obedience and deference to her husband. But that didn't mean she agreed with him.

"The people look to us to reassure them that they will prosper under our rule." Her mother turned to her, fixing her with one of her penetrating looks. "God favored your father and placed him on the throne. This finery is merely a reflection of that and reminds everyone of our power and position. Which is also why we cannot allow ourselves to appear weak and why I must put the needs of the kingdom above my own."

Edith nodded solemnly. She knew her mother was trying to explain why she stubbornly ignored her doctors. However, doubt festered. Had a council not voted to place her father on his throne? Did he not rely on the support of his lords and army to maintain power? There would be no need for such things if everyone truly believed that God favored him. Then again, God always tested his subjects.

This was how it always was with her.

Debating—if not with her tutors, then with herself. She strived to be a dutiful daughter but, at times, her contrarian, inquisitive mind made this difficult.

Her mother wrung her hands together on her lap, her eyes now closed in deep contemplation. Edith wondered if her thoughts turned once again to Edward, her eldest son. He had grown into a strong young man, but he had done little to distinguish himself either in politics or on the field of battle. When her mother was not berating him over some failure, she was praying that, should tragedy befall her husband, the council would elect him to be the next King of Scotland.

The doctor's return interrupted the silence that had fallen on the room. A servant carrying a pure silver chalice filled with the medicine followed after him. The doctor directed him to place it on the table beside the queen.

"After consulting with the others, we made a decoction of iris and honey mixed with spiced wine. This will help ease your coughs and help purge you of evil biles."

"Thank you, Doctor." The queen sipped the drink, her face a mask of calm contemplation.

Edith wondered how her mother could appear so stoic. Even if she stubbornly refused to acknowledge her illness, her husband was still riding out with an army. Wasn't she concerned at all? Or was she so certain of his success?

Their troubles had all begun months ago when her father had gone to England. He wished to find a peaceful but final end to the disputes over lands in Northumberland that rightfully belonged to her mother.

Despite a formal invitation, the English king had snubbed him, refusing to see him at all.

No longer trusting him, her father had come to Romsey Abbey, where Edith and her sister, Mary, had been studying with their aunt in England. He had whisked them away back to Scotland without warning or explanation, until they had crossed the borders.

Now he was preparing to take the lands by force. Even though he was a great warrior, Edith feared for his safety. Surely her mother did not wish for him to go through with this. Then again, perhaps she had tried and failed to stop him.

Edith would never know.

Queen Margaret was dressed in a gown of crimson red hemmed with a border of green embroidery. She wore jeweled rings on every finger and a gold chain studded with rubies from which hung a cross said to be blessed by the Pope himself. Then Edith placed the circlet on her mother's brow. It caught the light filtering through the windows and cast an ethereal glow about her.

Margaret, Queen of Scotland, beheld herself in the small mirror. She pinched her cheeks to bring some color and vitality to her face and then nodded, satisfied.

When her mother held out her hand to her women, they helped her to her feet.

Edith blinked. Her mother had indeed been transformed from a mere woman to something greater: a queen. Even her illness was hidden beneath the finery.

"We shall go to hear Mass in the chapel with my husband and pray for their safe return and victory," she said, with grave authority in her voice.

She took a step forward toward the door, then hesitated. With a look to Edith she held out her hand and added, "Daughter, you will walk by my side."

Edith rushed to take her hand. The others hurried to adjust their skirts and veils. In the commotion, her mother leaned toward her and whispered, "I need your help."

Edith braced herself as her mother leaned on her. Beneath the long sleeves and brocade of her mother's gown, she felt the tremor that ran through her as she gritted her teeth.

"Act as though nothing is wrong, Edith," her mother commanded.

They processed forward, the rustle of their fabric announcing them to the men waiting outside the chapel.

Edith's father, King Malcolm, stood in the center of the group. He was a tall man with wide shoulders and a long beard. His expression softened as he saw them approaching. His attention never wavered from Edith's mother.

"Good morning, my lady," he said. As he studied his queen, Edith could see unmistakable concern in his eyes.

"I've come to bid you farewell and pray at your side, my lord," Queen Margaret said, her voice carrying around the chamber so all might hear her. She released Edith's hand so she could turn to look at her son standing to the left of his father. As the eldest, Edward carried the expectations of their parents on his shoulders. Edith had never envied him until times like these when it seemed as though no one else mattered to their parents.

Margaret inclined her head to him as he stepped forward to kneel for her blessing. "Son, may God bless you."

The choir in the chapel began to sing. It was the sign to the congregation to take their seats for this special Mass.

No matter how often she heard the music, Edith never failed to be transported by the ethereal sound. As she kneeled on a cushion behind her parents, she closed her eyes and listened in earnest to both the priest and the music.

The sensation that all would be well filled her with such overwhelming joy that she smiled for the first time in days.

After Mass, they retreated to the great hall, where the royal family took their seats on a raised dais before all the court.

Servants carried in platters full of food, from roasted meats to stewed vegetables. Candied nuts and pies filled with preserves and mincemeat followed.

Throughout the meal Edith couldn't help notice that her mother ate little and grew paler.

At last her father stood and announced it was time to depart. He retreated to dress for the upcoming battle. Those who were riding out with his small army did the same, while the rest of the household assembled in the castle's courtyard to watch the departure.

Edith blinked as her eyes adjusted to the brilliant blue sky above them. The weather was mild, neither too hot nor too cold.

There had been at least four days without rain, which meant the roads would be dry and the travel for the carts laden with goods for the army would be easy. A princess usually did not concern herself with such things, but she had traveled to the south of England and back several times. Young as she was, she knew the hardships of life on the road. Rain might be a blessing for a farmer, but for a traveler it was a curse.

A bird of prey flew overhead. She looked up, trying to identify it from afar. If she believed in omens, she would think this was a good one.

Her father chose that moment to reappear, and she watched as he kneeled before his queen and asked for her blessing.

Queen Margaret placed two hands on his bare head, whispering prayers before moving on to do the same to her son.

Her father moved down the line to bid farewell to each of his children. There was no gravity in his tone as he commended each and every one of his younger sons before coming to his daughters.

"Edith," he said. "You are far too serious for such a joyous day."

Forcing herself to smile made her father laugh.

"You will become a great beauty one day. I shall be fending off suitors day and night."

Her smile faltered again. She had no desire to leave Edinburgh Castle. This was not lost on her father and he chuckled again.

"Do not worry. I would not part with you for many years. Even if the emperor himself was to write to me."

She grinned and bobbed a curtsy. Edith knew that if such a marriage were possible, her father would not hesitate to send her on the next ship leaving port.

King Malcolm imparted some last-minute instructions to the men he left behind at the castle before he moved to mount his horse.

From the corner of her eyes, Edith caught how her mother struggled to hold back another cough.

"Mother, perhaps you would like to go inside," she dared to suggest.

"There will be enough time to rest later."

What her mother said was true. It would take several days for her father to return even if the campaign went smoothly.

By now a small army had assembled in the courtyard.

The banners waved lazily in the soft breeze and the weapons of pikes, lances, and swords, which had been polished, gleamed in the sunlight.

Years ago a traveling bard had arrived at her father's court. He entertained the court over the Christmas celebration with his songs and poetry. The most popular performances had been the tale of King Arthur, some translated from Welsh, or so the bard had claimed.

Watching her father sitting up straight atop his warhorse overlooking the assembled men made her remember a stanza of poetry about the great king:

Men went to North with a war-cry,
Speedy steeds and dark armor and shields,
Spear-shafts held high and spear-points sharp-edged,
And glittering coats-of-mail and swords,
He led the way, he thrust through armies,

Five companies fell before his blades...

Her brother, Edward, fell in beside their father atop his own powerful steed and with that the warband set off, heads held high, certain of victory.

As the last man crossed under the drawbridge, her mother faltered.

"I need to sit," she said, her voice barely audible.

Edith panicked as she felt her mother go limp.

"Mother..." The words failed her as her mother fainted, falling to the ground though Edith tried to catch her.

The circlet fell from her brow hitting the cobbled steps with an ominous clank. The women of her household surrounded the queen trying to revive her. Soon a chair was brought for her and a few manservants carried her back to her rooms.

"Fetch the doctors," Edith called.

Her mother's companion, Alice, patted her cheek and handed her the fallen circlet. "We will take good care of your mother. Don't look so serious."

Edith hesitated on the threshold, watching as they took her mother away. Her hands tightened around the circlet she held.

"Will Mama be all right?" Mary asked, wiping the tears from her eyes.

Edith blinked away her own sorrow to look at her younger sister. Her brother had been led away by his nurse, only she had remained. Indeed, Mary had become her shadow ever since they'd gone to England together.

"Of course," Edith said, though her confidence was waning. "Father has hired the very best doctors for her. She just needs to rest."

Mary, only eleven, was already taller than Edith, but there was frailty to her. Thin as a reed, one would never guess that she could read and write in perfect Latin. Her cheerful disposition and gentle manner earned her the affections of all who knew her, but that didn't mean she was any less devious than Edith herself.

Over the years they'd grown close to each other. Perhaps it was their peculiar upbringing that had brought this about. Their parents love of study meant they had been eager to send their daughters to England to the excellent tutors at Romsey Abbey. There they had been educated more than most men, in languages, mathematics, and the classics. Certainly, they were oddities at the Scottish court.

Edith regarded her younger sister. Mary's brows were furrowed with worry and it prompted Edith to wrap a comforting arm around her shoulders.

She often forgot how different they could be. Whereas Edith thrived on constant change and adventure, Mary was happiest when her days were regimented and familiar. Their mother's illness and their father's hasty departure must have been shocking to her.

"We cannot dawdle. Will you write to our brothers?"

Mary nodded and Edith led her inside, only releasing her on the steps that led to the private solar.

"I'll look after Mother while you write the letters. There's no use fretting now and worrying about the future."

Mary gave her a baleful smile, perhaps amused by the way Edith took charge. "*Allez.*" Go.

Two

The room was dark and there was an eerie murmur of hushed voices as the ladies and doctors crowded around the queen laid out on her bed. Edith had to swallow down her anxiety. It didn't help that the windows were shuttered against the light and smoke from the fire in the grate filled the room. She forced herself to move and handed the circlet to one of her mother's ladies to be stored away.

Then her eyes darted around the room, searching for someone who could advise her. It was the figure of her mother's confessor, Turgot, the Prior of Durham, that caught her attention.

He met her gaze with his own. His smile, though strained, was warm. He turned back to Queen Margaret laid out on her bed, made the sign of the cross over her, and approached Edith.

"Princess Edith, your mother's fainting spell must have shocked you," he said. The godly man was never far from the altar and the scents of candle wax, frankincense, and myrrh were infused into his very being.

"I am. Is she —" Edith was at a loss for words. There was no sense asking if she was well or if she would recover. She knew the answer to such pointless questions already. "What can I do to help?"

The corners of the prior's eyes crinkled. "You are wise, child. But do not try to take the weight of the world on your shoulders. It might be too much for you to bear."

"I would rather run myself ragged than stand here like that useless chair," she said with some ferocity that surprised even Turgot.

"Beyond praying for her soul there is nothing the two of us can do. It is in God's hands."

Unable to accept this, Edith's mind whirled with possibilities. "Should we write to my father?" Her fingers were already itching to begin.

"I have sent a messenger. Sit with your mother. I am sure your presence would comfort her," the prior said, being far more patient and kind than he ought to be. He waited, hands clasped in front of him, for her response.

It was with a sigh that Edith relented, seeing not only the wisdom in his words but the truth in them too. "You are right. I must place my faith in the Lord. Thank you for your help, Prior."

"Fear clouds our judgment. Don't lose yourself in it. Now, I promised your mother I would conduct a special Mass for the safety of your father at Durham Priory myself." In a conspiratorial whisper he added, "And since your pious mother refuses to ask, I shall say special prayers for her health as well." He straightened up and left the room, taking his calm serenity with him.

Edith wished he had stayed.

She approached her mother's bedside and saw how a maid was wiping away the beads of sweat forming on her mother's brow.

"Does she have a fever?" Edith asked, fearing some new illness had found its way into the castle walls. Only a week ago a group of merchants had visited Edinburgh to sell their wares. The royal household had been treated to the sight of silks and brocades from far-off lands. But everyone knew travelers brought sickness with them...

"It's not a fever. She's exerted herself too much today," the maid whispered, not meeting Edith's gaze.

Her mother's eyes were closed, but her expression was twisted by pain. There was more to this than simply being tired. However, not wishing to argue, Edith nodded and took hold of her mother's hand. She tried to ignore how cold and limp it was. Such weakness was completely at odds with everything she'd known of her industrious mother.

After some time the doctors left and the ladies melted away or sequestered themselves in the chairs at the back of the room. Given the privacy, Edith said a private prayer and kissed her mother's hand.

Queen Margaret's eyes fluttered open and she turned her head to regard her with clouded eyes. "All this fuss over me." She tsked, then blinked as though coming out of a dream. "Edith?"

"Yes, it's me," she said, drawing closer to hear her mother.

Her mother looked surprised to find her there. "Why aren't you at Romsey Abbey?"

Edith bit the inside of her cheek. Had her mother forgotten that she'd returned from England months ago?

"Where is your father? I need to see him. Now."

Edith gripped her mother's hand tighter. "There's no need to fear. You will get better. The doctors are preparing medicine for you and they plan to bleed you. You are simply tired."

"Where is the king?"

So she forgotten he had ridden out to war. Edith didn't have the heart to remind her mother and so she said, "He is coming, I promise."

At that moment a log split in the brazier and a loud pop echoed in the room. Edith jumped in terror at the unexpected sound. An unsettling feeling of panic and doom descended on her, but she maintained her smile and kept hold of her mother's hand.

Her mother squeezed back. "I am glad. Read to me, Edith. Read to me." With her other hand she pointed to the Bible laid out on the table near her bed.

Edith ran to fetch it and, settling back on her cushioned stool, read in a clear melodious voice, hoping the words would comfort her mother.

Three days later, her mother was still unable to leave her bed. Edith refused to leave her side. She feared if she did, something would go horribly wrong. It didn't matter how much her younger sister might prod her or the older women of the household might argue with her. Like her mother before her, Edith straightened her back and refused to budge. She was a princess of Scotland. She outranked them all and she would do as she pleased.

One day after a priest said Mass, her mother had managed to eat some hot porridge. Edith could've cried with relief at this first sign of improvement. She was so absorbed in the task of watching her mother she didn't hear the commotion behind her until a hand touched her shoulder and made her jump. She glanced round, her eyes stinging with the effort, and saw that Turgot had returned.

"It is time for you to get some fresh air, Princess Edith," he said, with such authority that she found she was getting to her feet before she even realized what she was doing.

"I cannot leave her. She might need me," Edith said, feeling for the first time how tired she was.

The prior arched a brow. "You believe you are the only one who can help her? Lady, that is nothing but the sin of pride. But I am not here to lecture you. I see how devoted you are to your mother. So I promise to remain by her side and send for you the moment she wakes. What will she say when she sees you? She will have me whipped for not taking better care of you."

Edith struggled with herself before finally acknowledging that he was right. She retreated reluctantly to her rooms and ordered a chambermaid to fetch her hot water to wash, before changing her clothes.

Feeling refreshed, she took Mary up to the ramparts to stretch her legs. Her eyes, still strained from reading the Bible by candlelight, had to adjust to the bright morning sun. She breathed in the crisp air and felt herself relax.

It was then Mary said, "Duncan is on his way."

Edith came to a stop. Their half-brother lived far away from court. Older by more than a decade, they were practically strangers. What she knew was that he often quarreled with their father and he had banished them from court to avoid further trouble. "You wrote to him?"

"Not I." Mary shook her head. "I heard the steward telling the chamberlain to prepare rooms for him and his retinue. He must have heard that Mother is sick by now."

Edith mulled this over.

Who had told him? Did they have spies placed around the court? Or worse, did the nobles support him? One thing was certain, however: he was not riding all the way to Edinburgh out of kindness.

"And there's still no word from father? What about our brothers? Edmund, Edgar, and Alexander would surely—" Just then she saw a cloud of dust being kicked up on the road. A man was riding hard towards the castle as though his very life depended upon reaching it. As he drew closer, Edith squinted and could just make out her father's livery. "Guards, a messenger! Open the gates," she shouted.

All her prayers had been answered. Her father was coming home and all would be well again.

Edith didn't wait around to watch what was happening from afar but rather whirled around and started towards the stairs. She planned to be in the courtyard to receive him. A hand grasped hers, pulling her up short.

Mary held her firm. "You can't just storm down there. You're a girl. They will—"

Edith frowned. "I am the princess."

"Exactly, and a young one at that."

Edith was ready to argue, but she could see how the steward might bar her way. In her mother's apartments she held sway, but did she among the men? Could she trust any of them?

"Turgot. I will go speak to the prior. Surely he will help me. Come on, Mary. There's no time to wait."

They ran as fast as their legs could carry them.

When they entered their mother's sick room panting for breath, Turgot stood, surprised by the sight of them.

"A messenger is just arriving," Edith hurried to explain. "Will you come hear what he has to say?"

He looked surprised. "Certainly." His gaze flicked to Mary.

"And I will stay by my mother's side," she jumped in to say.

Edith squeezed her hand, knowing Mary would have preferred to come with her.

"Lead the way, Princess Edith," Turgot said, ushering her back toward the door.

In the courtyard, her father's steward had pursed his lips upon seeing her, but Turgot overrode his attempts to have her sent away. He might've argued more if the messenger hadn't chosen that moment to come riding in.

"I've traveled from Northumberland," the messenger called, as he slid from his sweating horse. He swayed as he tried to take a step.

"Someone fetch the poor man some water," Turgot shouted before another word could be uttered. He went forward and took hold of the man. "You must be tired. Come inside, eat and drink. Then tell us your news."

The steward went red in the face.

But Edith could see how wise Turgot's suggestion was. By now a curious crowd had gathered in the courtyard. Whatever news the messenger brought would spread through the castle and then the city below before nightfall. It was always better to keep your cards close to your chest, lest your enemies have time to plot against you.

But the messenger thwarted Turgot's plans.

He shook his head, and it was then Edith recognized him as her father's page, Angus. Edith's attention was drawn to the cut on the young man's face. It had been hastily patched up. With dread she realized the news he carried wasn't good.

Then he caught sight of her and ran towards her. Startled but unable to move, she wondered if he were an assassin. Thankfully, he merely fell to his knees at her feet.

Edith was close enough to see that the jagged wound had scabbed over, but showed signs of infection setting in. She'd seen plenty of wounds treated at the abbey in England and what happened when treatment failed. Perhaps the page was mad with pain.

"A curse on the English!" Angus cried out as if his heart had been wrenched from his chest. "Princess, the king is dead, and your brother too."

Edith was struck dumb. He went on, but his words fell on equally deaf ears. *The king is dead. The king. Her father. This made no sense. It couldn't be true. And yet. It must be.*

Wide-eyed and hopeful this was all some nightmare, she looked at Turgot only to find his serene face was taut with worry. The steward came forward and her gaze flew to him.

"What madness is this?"

For a brief moment Edith felt the faint flicker of hope

that there'd been some misunderstanding. That Angus was mistaken.

"I speak the truth," Angus said, holding out a folded piece of parchment. "A letter for the queen. It was his last..." He let out another cry.

Edith, too stunned to react, watched as the steward plucked the letter from the man's hand and tucked it into his pocket.

"We were ambushed...what remains of our party is riding back. They sent me on ahead. Their bodies...thank God we are able to bring them home." The page hung his head and wept.

This at last shook Edith from her stupor. What business did this man have crying like this when she couldn't allow herself to? And her mother. Edith swallowed hard. How would she react? What would they do? Who would rule now?

Anxiety bled into her sorrow. Her hands clenched into tight fists as she fought to keep her composure. The building pressure in her chest was growing too much to bear. She turned on her heel and walked as calmly as possible toward her mother's room. She would have to be told right away. Perhaps she might even know what to do.

Turgot caught up to her on the stairs.

"Princess, this news must have come as a great surprise..."

"It has. My heart is broken. Now I must hurry to my mother's side. The lords will have to be told, a new king chosen...my brother." She gave a shake of her head as she tried to cast off the haze that had settled on her to focus on what would happen now. "I must go."

"Princess." Turgot touched her hand. "These matters are beyond you. Your grief is great and you've suffered much these last few days. Let me go speak to your mother. You should rest and recover from this tragedy. Now is not the time to worry about the future."

"How can I not?" she asked, not bothering to be polite or demure. "Whoever is named the next King of Scotland will determine if I have one or not."

The prior's eyes widened. Perhaps he'd been unprepared for her worldly knowledge. She might be young, but she had studied and seen a great deal of the world.

"You are not without friends, Princess."

Edith nodded. "But will they protect us? Who will stand with us? My brother—Poor Edward is dead. He was the only one of my brothers who stood a chance of being elected king. Will the lords look favorably on Edmund? He is even more inexperienced." She bit her lip.

Turgot regarded her for a moment as if weighing his next words carefully. "Your allies must be warned. This is now a matter of urgency. We don't have a moment to lose," he said, letting out a sigh. "And yet, for all our haste, we might still fail. Princess, if you wish to help, then return to your mother and break this sad news to her alone while I slip back to my priory before I am noticed. Tell no one. The steward—he's loyal to the crown and Scotland. But he's wily and hates the English with a vengeance. He spoke out against your father marrying your mother. I do not know if you can trust him."

Edith nodded. Her father had always been the mediator between her mother and his steward. She doubted the steward, who hated the queen for her English blood, would be loyal now.

"Can you do this?" Turgot asked.

Edith needed to know more, but she felt his urgency and merely nodded. She watched for a moment as he hurried back down the stairs before turning to the daunting task ahead of her.

THREE

Her mother was awake, propped upright by several pillows while Mary urged her to drink some mulled ale.

As one they turned to look at her.

Edith curtsied, wishing she could send everyone but her family from the room without raising suspicion. Whose side would they all take? Would her father's death spark some fresh civil war for the crown? Edith forced herself to step forward.

"What is it?" Her sister set down the cup and took her hand in hers.

Edith's gaze fixed on her mother. With her sunken cheekbones and dark circles under her eyes, her mother looked more like a ghost than a queen. She shuddered at the thought before forcing it away.

"Father has fallen in battle and Edward with him." Only her mother's ragged breathing could be heard in the room. To fill the silence Edith felt it necessary to add, "We must rejoice they are now in the care of God and that we will be able to give them the funerals they deserve." Her vision was blurred by tears. Saying the words out loud had made them real. She reined in her grief, waiting for her mother to react.

When at last she did, her words were a pained whimper. "What tragedy has befallen us?"

"Mother, what shall we do?" Edith grasped her icy hands like a lifeline. "Please."

She never got an answer. Her mother turned her head upward and was muttering prayers under her breath.

Mary had begun sobbing and Edith could no longer hold back her own tears. She turned to her younger sister and they held each other as they cried. What would become of them?

Queen Margaret of Scotland died on the day the Masses for her husband and son began. Some priest had done his best to hastily embalm them and prepare them for lying in state while they waited for the great council of lords to arrive to elect the new King of Scotland. Now they hurried to prepare the queen. Was this a sign from the heavens that God was displeased?

Somehow, between the heavy hand of the high steward and Edith stepping into a role she was ill prepared for, they held back chaos from descending upon Edinburgh.

Every morning began as it had before.

The kitchens roared to life as the fires were stoked and bread laid out on great boards for the day. The servants ran about, completing the menial tasks that kept a grand castle from resembling a hovel. No one had time to be shocked. The king and queen might be dead, but that didn't mean the princess was allowing standards to fall.

After the death of her mother, the court was frozen until they watched the princess descend from her chambers dressed in black to attend Mass with her younger sister and two brothers beside her. The women of her mother's house now trailed behind her, their heads down, obedient to this new order of things.

After a lengthy service, they retreated to the great hall to break their fast. The thrones sat empty, but the royal family sat under the canopy of state on the high dais, reminding everyone that life must go on and if these four sprites could do it, so must everyone else.

They didn't know what it was costing Edith to keep her tears at bay and her hauteur regal.

She knew this could not last. Any day now the lords of the land, her brothers and half-brother would descend upon the castle. She would be forced to watch as they picked over the riches and titles like vultures.

But until then she had to make a show of strength.

As the daughter of a king she was set above others. Every day she had to prove herself. There were many who watched her, waiting to report on any misstep, any failure, as though that would prove her mother's line was unfit to rule Scotland.

The high steward was a man who preferred order. Perhaps he didn't approve of the way Edith was trying to fill her mother's shoes, but he knew this was all temporary and it suited him to have someone managing the women.

At first Edith had been worried that he would stop her

or forbid her from having visitors. All under some pretense that he was doing this for her safety. But he had not. It never occurred to him that she was doing anything but praying with her mother's former confessor and friend.

Edith had witnessed power before, in men and women alike. She'd seen how her father's mere presence captured everyone's attention. Or how a single word from the abbess had everyone rushing to obey her command. That sort of power drew attention, invited conflict and jealousy.

Now Edith learned of a different sort of power yielded by those who were often overlooked. It was a slyer, less noble power but one she appreciated nonetheless.

The high steward was in the great hall speaking to the chamberlain in hurried whispers when Edith entered. She didn't hesitate to join the two men, who bowed to her respectfully even though they could barely conceal their annoyance.

"Has there been news?" Edith asked in a placid, subdued tone.

"Nothing to concern yourself with, Princess," the chamberlain said.

Edith took a deep breath. "But if there are to be,"—she hesitated here, before settling on a word that felt safe—"visitors, I should be told. I can have the women prepare the rooms and ensure that everything is in good working order. I expect a great many are on their way here. Rather than constant shuffling of rooms as one lord displaces another for the best rooms in the castle, why not leave this matter to me?"

The chamberlain gaped while the high steward

regarded her suspiciously. Had she dropped the facade of the meek mourning princess too much?

"You should not be troubled with this, my lady," the chamberlain said. "We can manage."

Edith was ready to argue, but the high steward interjected. "Your brother is arriving with the Earl of Angus and his retinue."

Edith straightened. She knew this day would come, but she played the innocent. "Which—which of my brothers is arriving?"

"Prince Duncan."

"Ah. Excellent. I suppose his wife and family will be traveling with him." Edith didn't wait for any of the men to confirm this but nodded to herself. "Then I will be off to make preparations, ensure we have clean linen and..."

"Yes, yes." The high steward barely stopped himself from dismissing a princess of Scotland as though she were a maid. He found her irritating. Edith was sure he longed for the day when she would be forced back into obscurity. "You are most helpful, Princess. Thank you," he added, remembering his manners.

Edith's smile didn't quite reach her eyes, but if either man noticed they didn't comment or stop to wonder what she was really thinking.

The high steward was confident that order would be restored once a new king was crowned. And there was only one he could think of that would be suitable.

Days later, heralds and trumpets announced the arrival of her half-brother, Prince Duncan and his retinue. Edith, watching from the window in her mother's room, pursed her lips. She counted several carts and men, both astride horses and on foot. If he was merely here for the state funerals, then he would not have brought so many.

There was no mistaking this show of force.

A sharp knock on the door startled her. Fiona, her personal attendant, stepped inside.

"Princess, you don't have much time if you still wish to greet them in the courtyard."

Edith peeled herself away from the window. She allowed Fiona to plait her hair and tuck it beneath a wispy black veil. It matched the black of her gown, hemmed with a border of silver. She examined herself in the looking glass. With her hair pulled back into tight braids she looked austere, more mature and, she hoped, a force to be reckoned with.

All the inhabitants of the castle were curious about who was arriving. Many gathered to see and watch. These days information was more precious than gold.

Edith waited on the steps, surrounded by her women. To her right, at the forefront of the group, stood the high steward, barely able to contain his impatience.

The heralds rode through the portcullis first. Her half-brother followed after. But the grand vision of him in a black silk doublet astride a black stallion was not what drew Edith's attention. No, it was the man that rode in behind him.

Her heart leaped at the sight of Edmund, her eldest surviving brother.

A quick assessment told her he was not a prisoner. His smile was bright and he rode at a leisurely pace, glancing at the crowd that had assembled to greet the party.

Duncan leaped off his stallion and the high steward came forward to bow to him.

Her half-brother greeted him briefly before turning his attention to her. Still unable to comprehend the sight before her, Edith was happy she managed to maintain her posture.

He called something over his shoulder and Edmund stepped up beside him. Duncan wrapped an arm around his shoulders and brought him forward. They both bowed to Edith.

"Sister," Duncan said, as his eyes scanned her face. "What troubling times these are, but I am glad to be reunited with my kin."

She nodded, and remembering to curtsy, turned to her brother, Edmund. He looked sheepish. Unable to meet her gaze, and she knew with a fresh pang of worry that he had done something. Perhaps he'd made some secret deal with their elder half-brother that would benefit him.

"I am glad you have come so quickly. I hope the roads were good, brother," she said, maintaining her cool, detached composure.

Duncan let out a chuckle. "You remind me so much of your mother," he said, patting her cheek. "And they tell me you've been keeping yourself busy playing queen of the castle."

There was an edge of threat to his words.

"I am sure you are tired," he said. "You've had so much to do all on your own." He tsked, glancing around the court-yard again. "But now you shall have help. My wife has come with me. She will see to everything. You remember her, don't you? Lady Ethelreda of Cumberland."

"I never had the honor of meeting her. All I remember

is that Father didn't support the match," Edith said, unable to stop herself.

Duncan's smile widened a fraction. "Yes. Father feared I was marrying beneath me." He paused, as if he wished Edith would dare to contradict him. They both knew that their father had been worried he was plotting to strengthen his claim to the throne. Edith remained mute and so Duncan continued, no doubt hearing the soft footsteps of his wife behind him. "But my heart was smitten the moment I set eyes on my lady fair. Never had I seen such beauty." He turned to find Ethelreda had materialized behind him. Holding her hand, he presented her to Edith.

Decked in silk with gold rings and a heavy necklace, she was as richly dressed as queen. Yet, despite his words, Ethelreda lacked the poise and beauty he praised so highly. Before their marriage she'd been a great heiress and Edith suspected it was her wealth that enticed Duncan to defy their father.

"Sister," Ethelreda said, leaning forward to kiss Edith on either cheek. "How you have grown. The last time I heard about you, you were but a child heading to England. What adventures you must have had there. It is a tragedy you had to return at a time like this."

Edith gritted her teeth. "I prefer to think of it as a blessing that I could be here to attend to my mother in her last days and see my father one last time."

"Of course," Ethelreda said, her interest waning.

"Come, let's go inside, out of this sun and heat. There will be plenty of time to speak later after we have taken off these traveling rags and changed into something more suitable," Duncan said. His voice rang loud and clear. No one doubted who was in charge now.

Edith nodded; her attention turned to Ethelreda. "My mother's old rooms have been prepared for you. Would you like a bath?" Her eyes flicked to the dirt on Ethelreda's fine cloak.

"How thoughtful of you," Ethelreda cooed. She looked at her husband with an expression that seemed to say: *And you were worried.*

Edith and Ethelreda, followed closely by both of their maids, climbed the winding steps up to the private apartments the royal family used.

Edith took the lead and held the door open for Ethelreda.

Fresh rushes had been laid out and dried lavender and thyme strewn about so the room no longer smelled like the sickroom of a dying queen. Edith had ordered the new linen and furs for the bed. Tapestries decorated the walls and kept the chill at bay—but they were not the very best ones from the treasury. It was a small act of defiance on Edith's part.

Edith had hoped to stay in her mother's room herself but she knew Ethelreda would have said this was too much space for an unmarried girl. There was nothing she could've done to contradict her. So to save herself the indignation, she handed them over. Like a gracious princess should.

"There are plenty of hooks and chests for you to store away your things. The room is quite comfortable, neither growing too hot nor too cold in the evenings. If there is anything else you need from me, please ask," Edith said, eyes demurely downcast. She wanted to leave this place, find her brother Edmund, and discover what was going on. Had he not received her letters? And why was he in Duncan's company?

Ethelreda was still taking in the grand room, making a mental inventory of the riches that would be hers. It was just a matter of time. She busied herself studying the tapestries, gold crucifix and embroidered feather cushions.

"Thank you, sister." Ethelreda let out a contented sigh. "I was weary from my travels but now I find I am quite at ease. You've been so thoughtful to have this room prepared for me. Have you been looking after everything in the castle since your mother's death?"

Edith gave a curt nod.

Ethelreda's eyes filled with pity. "So much responsibility for one so young. Fear not. We, your family, are here to help now."

"I shall go—rest then," Edith said, deciding this excuse would suit her.

"Are you sure you do not wish to sit with me? My husband tells me you can read Latin. There is a book of psalms that I have tucked away somewhere in my chests. Perhaps you might entertain me..."

"I would love to. But I must speak to my brother," Edith said. Ethelreda's eyes narrowed.

"David is only nine. He has been quite lax about attending his lessons with his tutors." Edith smiled innocently. "And there is Mary to consider too."

Ethelreda let out a thin laugh. "I forget how fertile your mother was. There are so many of you that I lose count."

"I don't suppose you have news of my other brothers?" Edith asked, her attention fixed on Ethelreda's face.

She shook her head. "No. Quite the opposite. I wondered if they had sent any message to the castle. Maybe they wrote to you?"

"Unfortunately, no."

"Shame. Such a shame." Ethelreda was distracted by the glint of a copper chalice above the fireplace.

The servants arrived with a silver tub. Others carried in a great screen, towels and linens for this noble lady to wash away the stains of travel from her body and relax her weary muscles.

"I shall return the moment you call, sister." Edith bobbed a polite curtsy and left the room before the other woman could protest.

Rather than rush down the hall to check on her youngest brother, she swept through the corridors searching for Edmund. He was not in his room. Or rather the room he was traditionally assigned when he stayed in Edinburgh. So Edith had no choice but to go searching for him.

She walked with intent, eyes fixed ahead of her as though she knew where she was going, and no one stopped to ask her what she was doing.

Eventually she stumbled across him heading out of the keep.

"Edmund," she called out, trying to keep her voice quiet enough so it wouldn't echo around the stone hall.

He froze mid-step and it gave her the chance to catch up to him.

"Edmund, what has happened?" she asked, not bothering to dance around the issue.

"What do you mean, sister?" he shot back at her, brows furrowing with displeasure.

She bit back an angry retort and kept her features neutral. "Well, to put it lightly, I did not expect you to come riding to Edinburgh with Duncan."

Anger flashed across his features. He grasped her arm and pulled her along with him to a quieter alcove.

"What did you expect? That I would come riding here as fast as I could with an army at my back?" He shook his head as though the idea was some farfetched dream.

"That is exactly what you should've done. What I would've done had I been in your shoes," Edith snarled.

He scowled. "Then be glad you are not. What foolish notions have you been taught? Father should never have let you go to England. I told him so, myself."

"Tell me once and for all then, are you here as Duncan's supporter?"

"What business is it of yours?"

Realizing this conversation was going to devolve into them shouting at each other, she took a calming breath.

"It is my business. You know how Duncan felt about our mother. With Edward gone, you are now the eldest son. You have a strong claim to the throne. Yet you seem eager to give it up to support Duncan."

Edmund pulled the hat from his head, scrunching it in his hand. When he was younger, he might have thrown it to the ground and stomped on it.

"I have no land or army of my own," he hissed. "Edward

may have been able to raise an army. But me? I am lucky that Duncan seeks to make me an ally."

"He only does that because it's useful to him. But you are not without friends. There are many lords who would support you."

Edmund shook his head. "Too late. It was always going to be this way. If only my father had not married an Englishwoman."

Edith fell back as though she'd been struck. "How could you be so disloyal to our mother? She loved this kingdom and worked endlessly for us."

"For Edward," Edmund corrected, unfazed. "Enough of this. You are clearly overcome by grief. These matters should not concern you. Remember your place."

"If you think he will honor his promises of riches and lands to you, then you are mistaken." Edith stepped forward, gripping his forearm tighter than he had held hers. "As you say, you are useful to him for now. But the moment the crown is on his head you will be an inconvenient threat. At best he will keep you close to his side, allowing you to go on serving him like a dog. Once he has sons of his own, you will be a threat not worth keeping alive. Worst of all, you have doomed us, your siblings, to this fate as well."

She released him, flinging his arm away from her as though disgusted to be touching him, and left before he could retaliate. They would all pay for his cowardice. Hot angry tears pricked at the corners of her eyes, but she pushed them back.

FOUR

I n the dark interior of the chapel a priest was lighting candles and overseeing the servants dusting the rows of mahogany benches. Edith crossed herself and kneeled before the altar. The priest, used to the sight of the princess praying, went about his business, ignoring her. At length he retired and did not see another come in.

Turgot shuffled in, wearing unremarkable robes of black tied with a belt of knotted rope around his middle. He crossed himself and approached her.

After saying a quick prayer he whispered, "Is it true that your brother is supporting Duncan?"

"Yes," Edith murmured. Her hands clasped together tightly to keep from shaking and to maintain the illusion she was praying. "Have you heard from Edgar? He is our last hope, but I doubt—"

"We will pray, Princess. Fear not. But this complicates matters. How can the younger brother stand against both of his elders?"

"Edmund was always cowardly. At least that's what

Edward used to say," Edith added. Truth be told, she didn't know her brothers very well. They'd been parted at a young age and there had been such a difference in ages that they never spent time together in the nursery. Edward had been ten years her senior.

"You will be safe regardless, and for that we must thank God," Turgot stated as though he was hoping to convince himself of that fact.

"Assuming Duncan doesn't think we are threats. But before long we will become nuisances and then he will find a way to get rid of us."

"Given that your brother has befriended him, I think we don't have to worry about that for the immediate future. The council may vote against him. By now my letters will have reached your uncle Edgar Atheling in England. Perhaps the English king will intervene. Time will tell how this will all play out. You've done your best."

Edith wished she could've done more. She wished she wasn't forced to sit idly by while her future was decided for her, but neither did she have the power to raise her own army or influence politics. If only Edmund had not failed her. If only...

But when had wishing something ever produced results?

Edith bowed her head, praying for the souls of her parents and brother in earnest.

Over the next few days, the lords of the realm descended upon Edinburgh Castle. Her brothers, Edgar and Alexander, arrived with a small retinue of men from the north. It was too little and too late. Edith could see how shocked they'd been to discover that Edmund had cast aside his right to the throne.

It took all of Edgar's control not to come to blows with him in the great hall. Duncan had watched with a barely concealed smile as Edgar stormed off.

"He's full of rage, that brother of yours," Duncan said from his seat. Alexander was far more even-tempered and, seeing how the wind had turned, disappeared to drink in a tavern.

Edith, sitting nearby, glanced up to find Duncan had addressed the comment to her.

"Something I think all my brothers inherited from our father, even you," Edith said. "He was famously hot-tempered."

"And see where it got him." Duncan shook his head as if deeply grieved. "Well, what is past is past. I hope we can be friends. All of us."

"Of course, brother," Edith said, lifting her own cup of wine toward him. "To peace and fortune."

"Well put," Duncan said, and then stood, holding up his goblet. "A toast to peace and fortune." The men and women in the hall repeated the words. Duncan flashed Edith a smile. "I hope the next time Edgar graces us with his presence, he will be in a better mood."

She bowed her head, hiding the way her hands clenched into fists beneath the table.

With the court still in mourning, there was no singing and dancing after dinner and most retired early. Edith took her chance to slip away when Ethelreda left the great hall.

She found Edgar pacing around the solar and asked him to accompany her to the chapel to say a prayer.

Gallantly, he offered her his arm and led her to the second floor of the castle. They were unsure what to make of each other. But Edith had appreciated the foresight he had to come with men at his back, even though they were insufficient.

"You've met Prior Turgot, I assume," she said, leading Edgar over to him.

"I take it we aren't here to pray, sister," Edgar said ruefully.

"Not quite." Edith smiled. "Turgot was such a help to both our mother and father. Now he is in touch with our English uncle, Edgar Atheling."

Edgar's eyes gleamed. Perhaps he too thought that as a powerful English lord, he would surely save them. After the disastrous Battle of Hastings, he'd been elected king. However, he'd refused the honor, having the foresight to know he had neither the funds nor the men to fend off the Norman invaders. The former king had suspected him but still valued his wisdom. Over the years, he'd become a respected councilor. Their uncle had even been sent to Scotland as an ambassador for the English king. Surely he was a miracle worker to have not only survived the conquest but thrived.

Both Edgar and Edith shared a glance and felt that swell of renewed hope.

"And what does he say? He is friends with the English king. Would he support my claim?" Edgar tripped over his questions.

Turgot chuckled. "So impatient. No, young pup. He

wouldn't put his weight behind an untested prince such as you."

Edgar's chest puffed out, ready for a fight. His pride had been hurt too many times today to bear any further insult.

"That doesn't mean he won't help us in other ways, Edgar," Edith said, placing a hand on his sleeve. "Our uncle has promised we will always have a home in England. And who knows? Perhaps in the future he might help in other ways."

Edgar scoffed but did not pull away. "Scotland is my home."

"Of course," Turgot said, raising an eyebrow. "But you may not like it quite so much once Duncan is crowned king."

With a curse, Edgar spun on his heels and began pacing down the length of the chapel.

Princess and priest waited quietly as the heavy scent of incense helped to calm him.

He returned to them, smoothing a hand over his clean-shaven face as though wishing he had a burly beard to show the world he was a man.

"I will reach an accord with Duncan if I must. But I rue the day that Edmund was born. The coward." He spat. Then, remembering he was in the house of God, he sheepishly crossed himself.

There was something in his expression that reminded Edith of their father, and she felt the weight of his loss all over again.

The wolves were no longer content to lie in wait outside the gates. They were here. She felt them nipping at her heels. And their father was no longer here to protect them.

"You must try to put aside your hate. The earls of Moray and Atholl have all but announced their support for him. Who knows what he has promised them, but if you step out of line..." Turgot trailed off, but his warning was clear.

Edith rushed to add, "And at the banquet he all but told me to tell you that you were to dine with the family in the great hall. I don't know what he will do if you continue to defy him or be rude to him. You have neither the men nor the support of the lords."

"The Earl of Moray will stand with me."

"He is but one," Turgot said gently. "I have no doubt he is loyal to you, but he is a smart man. He won't fight a battle he has no hope of winning. We must wait for the tide to turn."

Edgar let out a frustrated growl but, to his credit, nodded. "I understand the wisdom of this, though it infuriates me."

"Find a way to put this energy to good use," Turgot recommended.

Edgar turned to Edith. "And you, sister. I am surprised to find you involved in these affairs."

Edith smiled. "I may never sit on the throne myself, but I do have a preference on who does. I have not been cloistered in women's rooms all my life and this has given me a unique insight into the politics of this land. Duncan may not see me as a threat, but neither will he have my best interests at heart when he seeks to marry me or even force me to become a nun. I imagine he will marry me off to some minor baron and ensure I live the rest of my days in obscurity."

"And that offends you? Perhaps you'd enjoy a quiet life in the middle of nowhere. You certainly wouldn't have to contend with these intricate power struggles."

Edith's eyes held her brother's. "I am the daughter of the King of Scotland, and the great Margaret of Wessex. Such a life would be unbearable."

He didn't smile or laugh at her words. Understanding passed between them without a need for words. He looked over his shoulder, checking to make sure no one had snuck up on them.

"We can meet here safely enough," Edith said, keeping her tone low. "I am known for coming here often to pray. No one will think anything of it if you do the same."

"Unlike you, I am not exactly known for my pious devotion."

Edith shrugged.

"Until I have more news, keep yourselves safe," Turgot said in a soft whisper and then, with a bow, left them.

Edith retreated back to the room she now shared with Mary.

Her sister was in bed, but the moment she closed the door behind her, her sister shot up out of bed.

"Has something happened?"

"Nothing for you to worry about," Edith said with a yawn. It was late. The sky outside their window was pitch black. Only the candle on the nightstand offered any light. "Where is Fiona? I would like to change out of this gown and go to sleep as soon as possible."

Mary rolled her eyes. "You are lucky you got to attend the feast. If I were you, I would stay until dawn."

"There was no dancing or merriment of any kind. Duncan was doing his best to play the part of king, while the other lords ate and drank to their hearts' content." Edith unpinned her dark veil and carefully laid it aside. "I hate not knowing what will come next. I fear nothing I do or say will matter. It's terrifying."

Mary climbed out of bed and wrapped her arms around her. "At least we have each other."

Fiona chose that moment to materialize, carrying a pitcher of steaming water in her hands. She bobbed a curtsy when she saw Edith had returned.

"It is late, Princess," she said, setting the pitcher on the table near the washbasin. "Do you require my assistance?" In the past Fiona had been their nursemaid, in charge of the princesses' well-being, and thus was used to ordering them to bed or to attend their lessons. Now that Edith was older it was no longer appropriate. Instead, Fiona turned to this gentle hinting.

Edith fought back a yawn and nodded. Before long she had washed and changed into a simple linen shift.

Both sisters trusted Fiona, but they felt uncomfortable discussing anything private around her. They settled in for the night, listening as she moved about the room, tidying up and preparing to sleep herself.

The following day King Malcolm III and Queen Margaret were finally to be interred at Dunfermline Abbey. A mausoleum had been prepared years ago. The abbey had been endowed by their mother and had been a special place for both of their parents. It had been their wish to be buried there. Unfortunately, it was a twenty-mile journey from the castle and they would have to set out at first light.

Women would not usually attend the burial of a king. However, as the queen was also to be buried, the women of the household joined as well. Priests, nobles, and their servants would follow the coffins in a solemn procession.

In this great train rode Edith and all her siblings.

Crowds of people lined the streets to watch them go, their heads lowered as the carts carrying the coffins of their deceased king, queen and prince went past. Many fell into step behind the procession while the priests prayed loudly.

It was a slow journey only made bearable by the fine weather and clear roads.

The bishop waited for them at the gates of the great abbey, wearing white robes and carrying a gold cross inlaid with precious gems.

The doors were held open as the coffins were carried inside.

The weary travelers entered the church to listen to the final Mass before the coffins would be interred.

Edith's eyes were dry as she listened to the words. Her spirit was lifted by the singing of the choir, mournful as it was.

At last her parents were laid to rest and Edith was happy that they were reunited together in death.

As the doors to the large stone mausoleum were shut, the finality of it all settled upon the crowd. Now they looked to the uncertain future knowing that tomorrow the party would return to Edinburgh and the matter of the succession would have to be settled.

The journey had taken the better part of the day and there was no question of them returning tonight.

Carts filled with food and tents had followed the funeral procession, as many would be forced to camp outside the town.

Thankfully, the royal family was allotted rooms in the abbey itself. Even so, Edith and Mary were forced to share a room with Lady Ethelreda and their maids. With six women crowded into a single room, the space felt cramped and the air hot.

Edith caught Lady Ethelreda glaring at them a few times. Would she find some excuse to have them removed?

Edith was too tired to argue but would not wish to be cast out to sleep in a cold tent.

"We are ever so grateful for the abbot to give us such comfortable accommodations. Unfortunately, we will have to leave at first light," Edith said to Mary but more for Lady Ethelreda's benefit than her sister's. "Let's try to get some rest while we can."

If Princess Edith could be patient, then so could the likes of Lady Ethelreda.

Edith wasn't sure if she slept a wink. She kept tossing and turning on her pallet even though the mattress was comfortable and smelled of fresh linen.

At the first signs of dawn, she nudged Fiona awake. The maid rushed to prepare fresh gowns for the day and changed both princesses. They plaited their hair with black ribbons and left the cramped chamber before Lady Ethelreda stirred from her own bed.

"That woman could sleep through a battle," Mary said with a laugh.

Edith bit back a smile but didn't correct her younger sister either.

They waited in the abbey to hear Mass, and Edith once more was transported away from her worries by the beautiful singing of the choir as they lifted their voices up to the heavens.

Piously, she prayed for the souls of her parents and for God to smile upon her family. *Let us find peace and contentment in the coming days.*

The journey back was decidedly faster without need for formality. It felt like a race to reach the capital.

This time Duncan rode ahead with his trusted friends and advisors, keeping Edmund close to his side. Ever since Edith exchanged heated words with Edmund, he hadn't sought her out or spoken to her beyond a mere nod of acknowledgement at mealtimes or at Mass.

She scanned the crowd for Edgar and Alexander and found them on the outskirts of Duncan's band. To Edgar's left rode the Earl of Moray. His expression had been fixed into one of cool displeasure ever since he'd arrived at Edinburgh.

The Earl of Moray disliked Duncan for being uncouth and arrogant. As a staunch Catholic, he privately considered Duncan to be an illegitimate bastard, and thus unable to inherit the crown. Duncan's mother and King Malcolm had been wed in the old ways without a priest to sanctify the union. This made her little better than a concubine in the earl's eyes. There were others who felt as he did, but they were willing to put aside their reservations because

Duncan was free with his favors and happened to be a powerful warrior.

Duncan knew what was said about his mother, but as his father had never treated him as a mere by-blow, he'd been able to claim these were merely malicious rumors spread by his enemies. Still, it didn't stop him from envying his half siblings. Before her death, his mother had never been crowned or respected. Meanwhile, Edith's mother was regarded as a pious queen, adding greater power to their claim. Had Edward lived, perhaps Duncan would never have been able to gather the support he did.

Edith considered Edmund from afar.

He'd always enjoyed the luxury and privilege of being a prince. But he lacked ambition and bravery.

Not that Edmund would ever confess this, but she had learned at last how Duncan had waylaid him on the road to Edinburgh. Until then, Edmund had felt he should be elected the next King of Scotland. But the moment his men were surrounded and his older, more experienced, brother had him cornered, he gave up.

During their last conversation, he had scoffed at her outrage without revealing the truth. She understood he must've felt a sense of deep shame over his weakness.

Would she have acted any differently? No. Probably not.

Yet, she couldn't forgive him for how loyal he was to their usurping half-brother. She turned her attention away from her brothers and spoke to her sister for the remainder of the journey.

Despite the sadness of the day, there was much to look forward to. For the first time in weeks there was to be a proper banquet and singing in the great hall of Edinburgh Castle.

Now that every ceremony to honor the old king had been observed, it was time to look to the future.

Tomorrow the lords would gather in the council chamber and deliberate on who would be the next King of Scotland. Once the decision was made, there would be an official crowning ceremony at Scone. This whole affair could be wrapped up by the end of the month. Thus, restoring a sense of stability to the realm.

FIVE

Edith, tormented by uncertainty and feeling more like a prisoner with Ethelreda insisting she not leave her side, found herself unable to cease worrying.

"Shall we not venture outside today?" Edith asked her sister-in-law. "It's such a lovely day…"

Ethelreda laughed. "And risk ruining our beautiful complexions? No." She shook her head. "You will learn to be grateful for my intervention. You have your looks to think about. What man would want you if you become freckled?"

Edith bit the insides of her cheeks, suppressing her indignation at such comments. "Then may I be excused to go pray in the chapel?"

Ethelreda smiled. "Oh, my dear. You take your devotions so seriously. Some might think you are quite the nun already. The past few days have been so trying. I wish you to remain by my side and keep me company. Come, help me with this needlework."

Edith could think of no other excuse to escape Ethelreda's watch and she worried if she pushed too much, Ethelreda would truly grow suspicious.

Mary was plucking lazily at the harp. She'd begun lessons in England, and though she was still a novice she played simple tunes pleasantly enough.

Edith took the offered seat beside Ethelreda and threaded the needle. She took up the work on the silk cloth. The material was a rich blue that glimmered in the sunlight that flowed in through the open windows. They were using silver thread to embroider floral motifs across the fabric while, Ethelreda was working on the outline of a lion.

"This is such beautiful work," Edith commented demurely.

"I shall wear it for the coronation," Ethelreda said, without thinking. Realizing how it must have sounded, especially in the presence of the other wives of the lords of the lands, she was quick to add, "For the blessed day. No matter who is to be crowned. Of course."

"Of course." Edith smiled, keeping her countenance sweet. Glancing around, she observed the sour expressions on many of the women's faces. They, at least, were not eager to have Ethelreda as their queen.

"I am told your mother's jewels are quite beautiful," Ethelreda said, as if it had just occurred to her.

"Yes. Many pieces came all the way from Italy."

"Imagine that," Ethelreda said, her eyes flicking from Edith to her sister. "You girls are so lucky to have inherited such a bounty."

Edith bowed her head over her work, pretending to be considering the stitch she had just made carefully in order to hide her smile.

"The jewels are part of Scotland's treasury. We were each given pieces as part of our dowry, but the majority will belong to the future Queen of Scotland."

"Ah." Ethelreda flushed. "Of course. Well."

Another woman hid a laugh behind a cough and Ethelreda's cheeks went an even deeper shade of red. Was it appropriate to be discussing jewels and who would be in possession of them before the crown was even on her husband's brow? Ethelreda changed tack.

"Not that this is the time to discuss such things. I cry when I think of your poor mother. Tomorrow I shall instruct my priest to say a special prayer for her soul."

"Thank you, Lady Ethelreda. I know she would appreciate you doing so very much," Edith said.

Her demure behavior pleased Ethelreda. She had done her best to play the part of the timid princess who couldn't possible cause any trouble. As far as they were concerned, that was exactly what she was.

By mid-afternoon, clouds had gathered and blotted out the sun. Ethelreda set aside her needle with frustration.

"We should have some candles lit. I cannot see a thing and I don't want to spoil this gown," she huffed.

"Perhaps some fresh air?" Edith thought to ask again. "For all of us? There is such a beautiful view from the tower —" Her words were cut off by shouts outside in the courtyard below.

Without waiting, she rushed for the window and beheld a strange sight. The men-at-arms patrolling the parapets were shouting something to the men below, who had begun assembling.

"Soldiers. Soldiers. We are under attack!"

Edith's breath caught. What was happening? Her hand flew to her mouth as she saw armed men on horseback charge through the courtyard. They were flying unfamiliar banners.

"Who is it?" Lady Agnes, wife to the Earl of Angus, asked, coming to stand beside her at the window.

"I don't know," Edith breathed.

"Has something happened?" Ethelreda's voice was shrill.

"There are armed men riding into the courtyard below. Why was the drawbridge left down and the gate not locked?" Lady Agnes hissed.

The other women flew to the windows to look down upon the scene developing. The guards on the battlements had crossbows trained on the intruders, but they were shot down by enemy arrows.

Edith gasped. Someone behind her screamed.

She moved away from the window, searching the group of women for Mary. Her sister was pale and frozen in terror.

Edith pulled her arm insistently. "Get away from the windows. They are firing arrows. It is not safe."

Ethelreda was uncertain about what she should do. She was still seated in her great chair, her embroidery work abandoned on her lap as she opened and closed her mouth, searching for words. She caught Edith pulling her sister away toward the door and shouted.

"Where are you two going?"

"Retiring for the night," Edith said through gritted teeth.

"Y-you cannot leave. You must st-stay," she stuttered. The sounds of ringing steel and shouts filled the room.

Edith ignored her, pulling her stunned sister out the door. There was chaos in the halls outside. Fiona came running toward them, eyes wide.

"Princess, we are under attack. Where shall we go?"

Edith bit her lip. Fleeing to her room wouldn't be any safer than remaining in her mother's old rooms with the insufferable Ethelreda.

"The chapel. We can claim sanctuary on consecrated ground." A thought struck her. "Where is David? He's too young to be caught up in all of this."

Fiona put a hand to her mouth. "He begged his nurse to take him to see the dancing in the great hall."

Edith cursed under her breath. "In all this chaos he will be lost or trampled or worse. Fiona, take Mary to the chapel and I will join you there once I find David. Now go." She pushed Mary into Fiona. The two didn't move. "Go," she half shouted at them.

Fiona was shaken out of her stupor and pulled Mary after her.

Edith took off at a run toward the great hall. Where there had been music and merrymaking there were now shouts of men fighting and screaming. Some were sounds of pain and Edith had to shut her ears and pretend she had not heard.

If anyone noticed her, they didn't say a word or couldn't spare her a second thought.

In the great hall, a table had been overturned. Food and drink were strewn around the room during the mad dash as everyone had fled.

"David!" Edith called. Outside the doors she heard the

fighting growing closer. "David, it's me, Edith. Are you here?"

There was nothing at first, but then she thought she heard a small whimper from the far end of the room. She rushed toward the sound, lifting the stained tablecloth to peer underneath. She found the huddled form of her youngest brother clutching a silver fork in his little hands.

"David, come out from under there. We have to go..." Edith pleaded, looking over her shoulder as she heard something crash against the shut doors of the great hall.

David shook his head.

"Please. I know somewhere safe we can go. You aren't scared, are you?"

David frowned a bit and shook his head.

"I thought so." Edith smiled patiently and held out a hand to him. "Come along."

It felt like it took a painstakingly long time for David to crawl out from under the table.

She patted his cheek. "We shall run for the chapel, and if we get separated for any reason that is where you shall go. Do you understand?"

"Yes," he said, his voice sounding so small.

Edith looked behind her. The sounds of fighting had grown louder. "We'll take the servants' entrance."

They took off at a run and disappeared down the back stairs just as the doors were flung open.

Gritting her teeth, Edith didn't turn back. She just ran, pulling her brother along.

"Keep going, don't look back," she urged him on.

At the doors of the chapel she ran through the large oak

doors and shut them behind her. Mary and Fiona were huddling by the altar and yelped when she ran in.

"It's just me," Edith said, panting. "And David."

Now that they were in the relative quiet and safety of the chapel, David found his voice.

"I should be out there fighting. I am going to be a brave knight."

Edith placed a hand on his shoulder. "I am sure you will be. One day. But you are only nine years old and haven't been practicing with the marshal for very long. You will have plenty of opportunity to prove your valor once you are older. I promise you."

Now that they had a moment to breathe, Edith regarded him for a moment. "Why were you alone?"

"Nurse ran the minute the fighting happened. There was music and an acrobat. Then all of a sudden shouting and I hid. She shouted for me but then ran off."

As Edith listened she felt herself shudder out of fear. She wished she knew more about what was going on, but there was no way for her to check. They would have to wait.

The noise in the castle dimmed at last. Edith wasn't sure what was better.

The door to the chapel was flung open and a group of armed men entered. Edith went pale, her heart hammered wildly in her chest, but she was proud she didn't scream or faint at the sight of them.

When they saw who was inside they sheathed their blades. A man pressed forward. He was tall and brawny. Edith gasped upon seeing his face. It was so much like her father she thought for a moment his ghost had risen.

"This is consecrated ground," Edith said in a loud steady voice.

The stranger regarded the four of them, before his eyes landed on Edith with a grin. "And you must be?"

"Princess Edith of Scotland. And you?"

He laughed at her impudence.

"Your father didn't speak of me often, did he? I'm your uncle, girl." He turned his attention away from her to regard the others. "I assume those two behind you are more of my nieces and nephews?"

"Yes. Princess Mary and Prince David." Edith stepped forward as though to block them from his sight. "Why are you here, Uncle?" She refused to address him by any formal title just as he appeared determined to disregard hers.

He ignored her, walking around the chapel as though making sure no one else was hiding there.

"You haven't seen that pup, Duncan, have you?" He turned to gauge her reaction.

Her mouth went dry, but her impassive mask didn't show the confusion his question sparked. Duncan was missing? Had he escaped? And what of Edmund, Edgar, and Alexander? She was desperate to know but doubted she could trust his answers and so decided to ignore his question.

"You stormed into the castle with armed men." Edith stopped short of accusing him of more.

Silence stretched uncomfortably long. He gave her a toothy grin. "Your father died. I rode here as soon as I could with these loyal men in tow and there was some—misunderstanding. But everything has been cleared up now."

Edith watched him, as wary as a cornered cat. She

didn't know what his intentions were but knew in the end if he wanted to, he could command his men to drag them out of the chapel and kill them. There was nothing she could do to stop him.

Her gaze studied the men with him. They were all heavily armed with swords and axes. The castle must have surrendered to him.

Duncan's goal had been to reach Edinburgh Castle and take control of it as soon as he could. He thought an initial perfunctory show of power was all he needed to do. Convincing Edmund to support him had only given him a further sense of false security. Ever since he arrived, his thoughts had been occupied with planning his coronation rather than fortifying his position.

"It is late, but the castle is safe once again. You shall all return to your rooms," her uncle commanded. "I will post some men to guard your door. These are troubled times." He said as if he wasn't the one that caused the trouble.

He had the awareness to look amused, and seeing Edith's sour expression only made his smile deepen. Perhaps he wished to goad her into saying something foolish, so he would have an excuse to throw her into the dungeon.

Edith was not so unruly that she didn't see the wisdom of backing down.

"How thoughtful you are, Uncle." Keeping her head high, she held out her hands for David and Mary. Hand in hand, they walked out of the chapel with Fiona following on their heels.

In the corridors outside the chapel there was no sign of the fighting that had taken place beyond an abandoned tray of food and a torn banner. Unsure if her mask of bravado would hold, Edith was grateful they didn't come across anything worse.

———

Tucked away in a single room, she forced everyone to go to sleep.

"Do you know what happened to my other brothers?" Edith asked Fiona in a whisper.

"No, my lady. Do you want me to inquire?"

Edith was tempted, but she could see the fear in Fiona's eyes. "I doubt my uncle would take kindly to you sneaking about. There's nothing we can do for now."

She wasn't sure how late it was, but at length Edith drifted off to sleep and didn't wake until she felt someone shaking her.

It was Mary. A night's rest had restored her spirit.

"What time is it?" Edith rubbed the sleep from her eyes.

"It's time for Mass. Or it should've been. There's chaos outside our doors and in the courtyard below. Strange men are patrolling the grounds and stationed on the parapets. But I don't know what we should do..."

Edith shot out of bed. Outside the sky was cloudy, which explained how she had slept so late. "I see you are already dressed. I will get dressed and then—" A knock at the door stopped her.

Fiona jumped, eyes going wide.

A few seconds passed and another knock came.

"Fiona, see who it is," Edith said, slipping out of bed and pulling on a robe.

Fiona did as she was commanded. Another maid stuck her head in the door. "You've been summoned to the great hall. All of you. Lord Donald commands it."

"Very well," Edith said. "We will dress first."

The maid shrugged and, since her message was delivered, disappeared.

"You should've asked her if she had any news about Edgar and Alexander," Mary said.

"I almost don't want to ask," Edith said, biting her lower lip. "I am scared, Mary. Scared of this uncertainty."

On the truckle bed their brother shifted in his sleep.

"Wake him, while I go get dressed. At the very least we can try to appear like royalty, not bedraggled peasants."

Surprisingly, the castle looked peaceful. The servants must have been ordered to spend the evening cleaning away the signs of destruction.

As they approached the great hall, she could hear raised voices. Armed men were stationed outside. They eyed Edith and her siblings.

"Who are you?" one man asked.

"Princess Edith. My uncle summoned us," she said, in her haughtiest impression of her mother she could manage.

She thought the other man sneered, but the door was pushed open and they were motioned to go through.

The commotion in the great hall quieted for a moment as all eyes turned to see who had arrived. Seeing it was only the younger of the royal children, talk resumed. Their uncle was sitting in the place that had always been reserved for their father, deep in conversation with a man she didn't recognize.

Now that they were here Edith was not sure where they

should go. They belonged at the high table in the place of honor, but approaching her uncle was the last thing she wanted to do right now. The crowd of men parted and she caught sight of her brother Edgar. Her heart leaped at the sight of him. He was safe. Thank God. But where was Alexander?

"Brother," David called out and ran to him. Edgar placed a hand on his head.

"Are you unharmed?" he asked, keeping his voice low.

Edith, having caught up, nodded. "Where is Edmund?"

Edgar's fury was unmistakable. Edith feared the worst. "Was he killed in the fighting?"

Edgar shook his head. "All things considered, very few men were killed. Most surrendered the moment it was clear that we were outnumbered and caught unaware. There was no point trying to mount a defense. We were defeated before the fighting even got underway."

"And Edmund?"

"Fled. With Duncan. The moment they heard the call of alarm and saw the number of men, they slipped out the servants' entrance, stole whatever horses they could get their hands on, and left us to the wolves," Edgar said.

Edith's eyes widened in disbelief at this tale.

"David had been in the great hall at the time. Did he not even stop to think about his youngest brother?"

Edgar's expression softened and he looked down at his youngest sibling. "Evidently not. You shall find I am not so quick to abandon you. Alexander disappeared into the city two days ago. Hopefully he has the sense to stay hidden."

Mary patted David's back. "Why has Uncle come?"

"The crown," Edgar said, looking over his shoulder.

"There's no other reason. Conveniently, he managed to trap all the great lords in one fell swoop too. Find something to eat. In these uncertain times we don't know when our next meal will be."

"I am not afraid to fight," David said, finding his voice. He wanted desperately to prove to his older brother how brave he was.

Mary put a hand on his shoulder as though to silence him.

"And I am sure we will make a great soldier out of you yet," boomed the voice of their estranged uncle. He had made his way over to them, his lips curled into a satisfied grin. "Nieces, nephews, come sit at my table. You are family. You should be honored as such."

Edith bit her cheek at the indignation of such an invitation, but they had no choice.

Their uncle clapped Edgar on the back hard enough to make him cough.

"Not quite the family reunion I envisioned, but I hope everything will be forgiven in time."

They ate in silence, observing the great lords and their ladies arranged about the hall. Bread, hard cheese, and watered down wine were served to them. Such fare would've been considered too simple to grace her mother's table, even in Lent when meat was forbidden. However, given the horror of what happened, Edith was grateful for even this. She wondered if this was just another example of their uncle asserting control.

Edith caught snippets of the hushed conversation Donald was having with Edgar.

From the sounds of it, he was trying to pry information

about Edmund's and Duncan's whereabouts from him. Did he know where could he have gone? Who were Duncan's supporters? Edgar, who even now wouldn't betray his kin, evaded the answers as best he could. Thankfully, Alexander was not mentioned.

Was this what their life would be like from now on? Kept under lock and key until someone set them free? Treated with the smallest modicum of respect.

Edith willed herself to be calm. Looking around the hall, she noted grimly that Ethelreda was still in attendance, her face white and her mouth pressed into a thin line of displeasure. So her husband had abandoned her too. She had gone from being queen in all but name to being a valuable hostage. That was if either her husband or uncle-in-law felt she was important enough. Personally, Edith didn't believe that Duncan would risk his own neck for hers.

By the end of the day a council was called to settle the matter of succession in Scotland once more.

Unsurprisingly, her uncle Donald, who'd stormed the keep with a band of seventy loyal men, won the vote. Edith watched from the sidelines as the great lords of the land kneeled before him and swore fealty. Many were doing so under great duress and she doubted any peace would hold. Many of the earls were proud men who would never forget this slight.

As arrangements for the coronation were made and she and her siblings were ordered to return to their rooms.

In time, they were given more freedom. David could even resume his lessons with his tutors. Edith could spend her days sewing with the ladies of the castle and looking after household affairs and her uncle didn't interfere, but they weren't allowed to ride out or go anywhere without one of his trusted guards present. Whether she was walking in the orchard or the herb gardens with her sister Mary or sewing with the marshal's wife, there was always someone watching. Ready to report if she took a step out of line.

Only Edgar was kept confined to his rooms and when he was allowed out, it was only in the presence of his uncle. Edith never got another chance to speak alone with him again.

Their uncle had years of experience under his belt and while he decided what he would do with them as he hunted the kingdom for Duncan and Edmund, they'd be safe.

Six

The temperature shifted from tepid to a biting chill. The firewood was being rationed and Edith was often forced to wear several layers of clothing.

Her finer silk gowns and chemises were laid aside in favor of thick wool and furs.

Had her uncle decided to let them freeze? Or did he hope they would catch their death in the frigid castle? She'd always complained about her days spent studying at Romsey Abbey in England, but now she longed for those structured days. She'd been unhappy for many reasons, from her oppressive aunt to the long hours of monotony, but neither had she been afraid for her life.

Edith couldn't help feeling she was playing a game where the odds were stacked against her. Every night she struggled to fall asleep and every morning she woke with a jolt, panic rising with the sun.

Her only reprieve was the quiet of the chapel where the

priest murmured his quiet prayers and the heavy scent of burning beeswax and incense soothed her anxieties.

In the past they might have journeyed to the abbey in Edinburgh, where a choir would've sung during Mass, but her uncle had forbidden them to leave the castle.

Among the storms and deadly cold of winter, her uncle was crowned. Edith moved like a shadow of herself, not entirely aware of what was happening around her. Duncan and Edmund had still not been found, but there were rumors they were gathering an army to challenge their uncle.

One morning as she entered the chapel she was surprised to find Turgot praying before the crucifix, his head bowed in deep concentration.

She kneeled and waited, saying her own prayers, even as her heart leaped at the sight of her mother's advisor and someone she had come to regard as a friend and protector.

"Princess Edith, are you well?" Turgot asked, once he had made his obeisance and crossed himself.

"I am, sir," she said. "But I long to know what is going to become of us. My uncle is now crowned and though he hasn't mistreated us, it is clear he sees us as pests. I worry he will lose his patience with us one of these days."

Turgot nodded, unsurprised to hear this. "I have bribed one of the guards at your brother's door. We were able to converse. He believes, as I do, that you and your siblings have no choice but to flee Scotland for the safety of England."

"That would be impossible."

"Not entirely. The king is still shoring up support among the lords and hopes to discover Duncan. Soon he will ride out with a small army. Your uncle Edgar Atheling is already in the city below and your brother Alexander is safe with him."

Her eyes widened with shock. She had not heard anything about his arrival.

Seeing her disbelief, Turgot explained, "He came under cover of darkness, disguised as a well-to-do merchant. He is keeping a retinue of men and horses near the border of Scotland, waiting to spirit you to safety. If you agree to our plans, of course."

Edith fiddled with the hem of her long sleeves. There was a rip that would need to be repaired. "I don't know if we have much of a choice. At best, my half-brother succeeds and takes the throne for himself. If that were to happen, our circumstances wouldn't improve. I agree with Edgar. We must flee to England. But we are all watched day and night. What shall we do?"

Turgot smiled benignly. "Leave that to us. Your uncle is on high alert at the moment but there will come a time when he lowers his guard."

"That may never happen," Edith said, unable to help the frustrated edge to her voice.

"It is in God's hands. But I believe we should have an opportunity after Christmas. By then King Donald should be too distracted with other matters to worry about you children. Remember, don't act like you are preparing to flee. I must also warn you that we will have to travel light. Bring only what will be useful or of value. Jewels, coins, warm clothes."

Edith nodded, already yearning for the comforts of home she'd have to leave. Her parents had always been generous with their children. She had soft chemises and gowns of every color. Not to mention there was always food in their bellies and a warm fire to sit by. Fate had snatched away a bright future, but Edith refused to be passive as the tide of fortune ebbed and flowed. She was prepared to pay any price if it meant freedom and safety for herself and siblings.

Now she wished they didn't have to wait until the New Year. Even as the prospect of fleeing in the dead of winter scared her. And if they were captured on the way? What then? She swallowed down her fear. They had no choice. This was the risk she would have to take, and if she paused to consider, she knew she would do so gladly.

"We must trust in God," Turgot said, reading her thoughts.

"And our plan. Amen," Edith said, crossing herself.

It played out much like Turgot had predicted. The first time her uncle had left Edinburgh, they were ordered to stay in their rooms with guards posted at the doors. The excuse, as always, was that the king was concerned for their safety.

"With rebels roaming the countryside I shudder to think what may happen if they were to get their hands on you," King Donald had said, shaking his head.

Edith wondered how he expected the rebels to even breach Edinburgh Castle's walls. The gatehouse was kept locked, and any other entrances in and out of the castle were heavily guarded. He wouldn't be making the same mistake as Duncan had, allowing security to grow lax.

Throughout all this, Edith felt it was best to keep her younger siblings ignorant of Turgot's plan. Not only was she worried they might accidentally reveal something, but she felt they deserved to be as carefree as possible.

On Christmas Day, King Donald allowed them to leave the castle to celebrate Mass at the Cathedral. It was the first time in weeks, that Edgar was allowed to leave his room. When Edith embraced him in the courtyard, she whispered, "We shall leave soon. Be ready."

He squeezed her hand to let her know he heard her.

"Why have we been released from our cages?" Edgar said, as they separated while they waited for the stablehands to bring their horses.

It was Mary who had the answer. "There are rumors around the country that Uncle has killed us."

Edith's throat went dry. "What? Who told you this?"

Mary shrugged. "It's just what I heard. I was sewing with the women and I heard them whispering."

Edith shared a look with Edgar.

"Well, don't worry about it. We are above listening to such petty gossip," Edith said.

"Yes. I know." Mary pouted. She hated having her fun ruined.

The more Edith thought about the rumors the more terrified she became. What if people, after being shocked by such tragic news, grew accustomed to the idea? Would it inspire their uncle to act at last? After all, if he was already being accused of the crime, he might as well commit it.

Once Duncan and Edmund were caught, Edith and her remaining siblings would be the only ones left with a claim to the throne. Killing them would ensure that there would be no one left to challenge him.

With the future so uncertain, Edith often wondered if her imagination was running wild.

"All will be well," Edgar said to them before he was called away by their uncle.

They processed into the church like a tight-knit loving family. Crowds of people had gathered to celebrate this auspicious day. It took all of Edith's resolve not to search the crowd for her other uncle that had come to whisk them away to safety.

As the Mass began she thought often about her father's past. There had once been three brothers and when the old king died, their uncle had taken the throne by force. He had wanted his nephews dead, and so to keep them safe, their mother had sent them into hiding. One to Ireland, one to England, and one to the wilds of Scotland. It had been her father that emerged the victor after many years of civil war and unrest.

She knew little about the nature of his first marriage, but as far as she knew her father had been a good man and a just king. It was evident in the way he had loved and cared for Duncan even after his second marriage. As for governing, he'd always placed the needs of his people first, never overtaxing them and always defending their rights. In return, they loved him. The outpouring of grief at his funeral made that clear.

The choir sang an "Ave Maria" and Edith felt her heart lift with the music. She prayed her father and mother were at peace. A sense of contentment swept over her as the music crescendoed and she felt assured all would be well.

After Mass, the court retired back to the palace for a feast.

She and her siblings were not invited, but they were served pheasant stewed with raisins and figs for dinner with copious amounts of cakes and pies for dessert. It was a decadent meal.

In the privacy of their apartments, Edith pulled out little gifts for her younger two siblings.

"It's beautiful," Mary said, holding up the gold pin to the candlelight. A sapphire sparkled and caught the light.

"It was my mother's. I took it from the treasury. One of her smaller baubles that I'm sure wasn't noticed."

"When did you manage to do that?" Mary asked her incredulously. They were never allowed to go anywhere without an armed guard and maid present.

"Don't worry, I cannot walk through walls or make myself invisible. I managed to snatch this while Ethelreda was examining the coffers." Edith smiled. "She was so greedy that I worried we wouldn't be given anything that was left to us in mother's will. I thought nothing of it at the time but—now I am glad I took them."

"I like mine too," David said. The sold gold ring he held was stamped with Scotland's sigil. It was nothing compared to the chains of pearls and gilded silver that could be found in the treasury. However, Edith hoped wherever life might take him, it would always remind him of who he was and what his parents had worked for. She looked down at the gold band encircling a polished lapis lazuli stone in her hand. It had been one of her mother's favorite pieces, now it belonged to her.

"We are the royal family of Scotland," Edith said, taking

on a serious tone that she hoped would make them take her words to heart. "It is our duty to look after the land and our people. Let these small baubles always remind us of that."

"Thank you, sister," Mary said, bobbing her a polite curtsy.

David was far less formal and hugged her round the middle. "When it's my birthday, can I have a falcon? One like Duncan's. It was big and flew so fast. It always caught its prey."

"How would you know that? He never took you hunting," Mary said, incredulous.

"I know," David said, his temper rising. "But I went to the mews and asked which was the best. I remember it had dark wings. Besides, Edgar said I have an eye for these things."

Mary opened her mouth to argue, but Edith, sensing more of an argument brewing, placed a hand on her siblings' shoulders.

"Let's get ready for bed."

Now they turned as one, allies against her.

"Not yet."

"It's still early." They whined.

Edith arched a brow, feeling far older than her years. Seeing their sad faces made her wonder why she had ever taken on the role of mother.

"As long as you stop arguing, I will play the harp and we can relax."

"Very well," sniffed Mary. "Though I play much better than you. Everyone knows this."

Edith rolled her eyes. "Then you can have that honor and I will sit by the fire roasting these chestnuts." She pulled out the treat from the pocket of her robe, holding back a laugh at the hungry gleam in their eyes.

"On second thought, I'd be happy to give you the chance to practice." Mary grinned.

You are very generous indeed," Edith said, rolling her eyes before handing the chestnuts to her.

As she fetched the harp, she watched her siblings argue over which ones would be theirs but quietly so she might not hear and scold them further.

Fiona returned with a pitcher of fresh water. It had been made clear to her that she was only able to keep her post if she understood that she was serving King Donald, not the orphaned royal siblings. Yet, she was still loyal to the children and had not told the king about the little treasures Edith had kept hidden away. To her it was innocent fun.

What Fiona didn't know was that Edith had hidden away more than a few trinkets. In her trunk that held her winter cloak and furs, there was a false bottom. Inside, Edith had saved a small purse of coin, pearl hairpins, silver forks, and a few other precious items. These had been hers before her uncle had deprived her of all her valuables. Perhaps he was more suspicious of her than he let on. But just as likely, he was desperate for funds to keep his army well supplied and to buy the loyalty and support of those who could be bought.

Edith didn't have to put on a show of displeasure as her red cloak trimmed with ermine disappeared one day, nor when her jewels, the ones that she had not hidden away, were inventoried and later confiscated. They hadn't touched the precious gold crucifix that hung about her neck, though the clerk had eyed it for a long time.

"It was given to me by my mother, and blessed by the bishop to keep me safe," Edith said, any flowery courtly language failing her at the thought of losing such a precious thing.

Deciding that taking such a godly item might imperil his immortal soul, the man had left it to her. After that, Edith had hidden it away. The next person to come looking for more things to sell might not have such qualms.

Poor Edgar was moved from his room to some other secure location in the Castle. She wasn't even sure in what condition he was kept in. She had asked her uncle if she and her siblings might be allowed to visit him, but he had laughed.

"Don't come to me with such foolish requests," he had said, with a shake of his head.

"I know you fear for our safety and cannot bear to let us out of your sight. You are truly a kind and loving uncle to us poor orphans. But surely, as every day your power grows, there's no need for such caution," Edith replied.

Her uncle looked stunned. A mixture of amusement and anger twisted his features. But there was nothing in her tone or comportment that would show she was being insincere. At last her uncle's eyes glinted with amusement and he tilted his head in acknowledgement of her skillful arguments.

"He should be glad he's kept in such princely apartments. There are other places he could be put for his protection." He paused. "The dungeons of this castle, for one, are world-renowned as being impenetrable, though perhaps not as comfortable."

Edith wasn't one to give up so quickly. Demurely, she

kept her eyes downcast. "Then, perhaps soon, when the realm is at peace, you will allow him to attend the jousting tournaments."

Her uncle, growing annoyed, waved his hands as though to dismiss her from his side. "Yes. Yes. Perhaps in the spring. Off with you. I don't want to hear another word on the subject."

Edith curtsied politely and retreated to the chapel.

Turgot was already there. When she kneeled for his blessing, he slid a piece of paper into her hand.

She didn't dare read the message until she reached the relative privacy of her rooms. With her uncle's spies in and out of her room, Edith set herself up by the window with her sewing. Needlework had always brought her immense satisfaction. The fine patterns and motifs she could create with something as basic as thread and needle never failed to amaze her. When she was younger, her mother never had to force her to practice.

Now she pulled out the linen shift she'd been working on. Over the last few weeks, she'd been busy embroidering entwining vines and leaves in a symmetrical pattern around the neckline. Edith focused on her work as she waited for attention on her to wane. Only then, under the pretext of searching her basket for a particular color of thread, did she unfold the scrap of paper.

If you find your worries burning. Come to the chapel.

The message was innocuous enough. Had it been discovered, it would've been easy to dismiss it as merely a note of reassurance. Edith only hoped she wasn't wrong about its meaning. But one thing was unmistakable: the time had come. They were fleeing this cage.

Glancing out the window, she saw that snow had begun to fall. She shivered as though she was already trudging through the snow. Would it impede their escape?

As evening approached, Edith put off getting ready for bed. Despite Fiona's yawning, she kept her siblings up playing cards and asking Mary to play the harp. After a time even Mary complained.

"Should we not go to sleep? I am exhausted."

"No. It is New Year's and we must mark the occasion. It's important."

Mary rolled her eyes, but then she caught Edith's pointed look and stilled.

"Another song then," she said, her tone more chipper than before.

David wasn't so quick to catch on. "I tire of playing."

"Have you played chess before?" Edith asked making a silent prayer to the saints to grant her brother patience.

"Yes."

"Then let's play a game. That should interest you. There are knights, kings, and queens all fighting for control."

He scowled. "I know. But it's not so fun."

"Well, we shall play anyway."

A maid came in to clean the hearth of ashes.

"We'd appreciate more candles," Edith said.

The maid eyed her. "It is very late—"

Edith put on her most imperious expression. Who was she to question a princess? Then all of a sudden they heard a distant cry.

"FIRE! FIRE!"

Edith screamed and pretended to faint, falling flat on the floor.

She remained there as the maid came to inspect her.

Mary pushed her away. "Go. Go get the doctor."

"There's a fire. We should..."

"Yes, go," Mary said, anything to get her away.

Edith's eyes conveniently fluttered open. She made a great show of being weak and putting her weight on Mary to help her get to her feet.

Fiona, who had been dozing on a stool, reached for her. "We must leave the castle. It's not safe." She peered outside and pulled back to see the thick black clouds of billowing smoke.

"I can't make it down the stairs," Edith said, faltering. "Get help. I can't—"

"I will!" Fiona called out and ran out the chamber doors. The guards were gone. Likely they'd gone to help put out the flames. After all, what could two princesses and a prince barely old enough for the schoolroom do?

The moment Fiona was out of sight, Edith made a miraculous recovery.

"We are escaping," she said to her two younger siblings. "Put on your heaviest cloaks and bundle up as much as you can." She rushed to her hiding spot. She wished she could take the forest green cloak with her, but it would mark her out. Instead, she found a plain black one she'd commissioned while she was in mourning for her parents. It was lined with fur and thick. Then she grabbed the treasures she'd accumulated and threw them into a small satchel. This was a far cry from what her inheritance was supposed to have been, but there was no time to dwell on that.

Turning around, she found that Mary had put on a cloak but was still wearing her silk slippers. "Change your shoes. We must hurry."

Thankfully, David had a fresh pair of thick leather boots that would keep the snow at bay. Edith could only hope they'd be able to ride out of the city rather than walk.

Then, without a second glance, she threw open the door to their chamber and the trio fled. The halls were darkened and smoky, but holding her cloak over her mouth, she relied on her memory to walk to the chapel.

"Hurry," Turgot said, not bothering with any social niceties the moment he saw them.

"Where is Edgar?" Edith glanced around the darkened chapel.

"He's making his escape a different way. Come along, there's no time to lose."

From the priest's quarters they were taken through the servants quarters. They kept their heads down and hurried along, following Turgot. No one looked twice at them.

Outside near the stables, Edith looked back to see smoke billowing out of the great hall.

"Into the cart. I'll hide you under the sacks of cloth," Turgot urged them. A mule was already harnessed to it.

David scrunched up his nose, but Edith pushed him forward.

"God bless you, children," Turgot said, making the sign of the cross over them. He placed the blankets and bolts of cloth over them. They'd gone from the heat of their room to the brisk cold night air. Now they were smothered once again.

"I can't breathe," Mary whined.

"Hush. All will be well," Edith said with a confidence she didn't feel herself.

The cart began to move and they did their best to not make a sound. Turgot was stopped by the guards at the gatehouse.

"Let me through. I don't want my goods to be burned."

"We are getting the fire under control now," the guard retorted.

Edith didn't have to see Turgot to imagine his scowl.

"These are bolts of Flemish wool. Do you think I'd take the risk? My abbey cannot afford the cost."

"Very well," the guard said, relenting, but not before he lifted a few of the bolts of cloth to see if the priest was hiding anything. His search wasn't extensive and Edith breathed out a sigh of relief as they set out again.

The cart rolled down to the city below, picking up speed as Turgot urged his mule onward.

"Your uncle is waiting for you at my abbey. Your brother will be meeting us there too. If all went well," he called down to them.

Edith's hand found Mary's and squeezed tightly.

Soon this nightmare would end.

Turgot's priory was on the outskirts of Edinburgh far from the castle. It had taken them a good hour, if not more, to travel here. They didn't dare leave their hiding spot in case someone spotted them.

At the priory the candlelight shone through the window. Turgot stopped the cart and another priest came to help unload the bolts. Once enough were removed, Edith, David, and Mary were able to sit up and slip down into the crunching snow.

"It's so cold," Mary said, clutching her cloak around her.

Snow was still falling, but it was wind that pierced through the many layers of clothing they wore.

"Inside," Turgot said. "I will have Father Benedict brew one of his famous tisanes for you and you shall have a bite to eat before you set off again."

He herded them inside.

The priory was a plain stone building. It was a productive one that sold a variety of goods and spiritual services. Many priests here were trained illuminists. They worked with precious parchment and painted embellishments on each paper as they copied out the words in painstaking detail. Then there was the farm and livestock that sustained them. In the distance, Edith could even hear the bleating of sheep.

Turgot took them through the inner courtyard to the dining hall.

A strange sight greeted her. Armed men were gathered around a table. They wore no distinguishing livery on their breasts or anything that might mark out who they were.

They looked up as one when Turgot entered with them.

"Edgar! Alexander!" David called out, being the first to spot his older brother. As he stood and approached them, Edith got a good look at him. He looked happier than he had at Christmas. His appearance was a bit disheveled, but apart from a bit of soot on his face, he looked none the worse for wear.

Edgar put his hands on David's shoulders, looking over his younger brother to make sure he hadn't been hurt. To Edith and Mary he gave a kind smile and nod.

Alexander looked thinner but happy nonetheless. Once

Edgar had finished inspecting them, he came forward to embrace his sisters and youngest brother in turn.

Edith's attention was already drifting away to the man who came to stand behind him. Their uncle Edgar Atheling.

"Uncle." Mary ran forward and, perhaps overcome with emotion, threw her arms around his middle. "Thank you for coming."

If he was surprised by the unseemly show of affection, he didn't show it but merely patted her back. During their stay in England, he had often visited them while they studied at Romsey Abbey. He'd thwart Cristina's strict rules about decadent food and brought them all sorts of delicacies from the court, from gingerbread to honeyed dates.

"It's good to see you all again," he said. "A year ago, I would never have dreamed all my sister's happy planning would've ended like this. I am sorry to have missed her funeral and that of your father's, but I see now that it was for the best. Has Turgot told you? We cannot linger. Your uncle Donald is a clever man. By now your escape will have been noticed and he will send men after you."

"What do we do now?" Edith asked.

"I have horses ready and men to guard us. More are waiting at the border. But we cannot rest until we get deep into England," he said. Then, eyeing the two girls, he snapped his fingers.

One of his men came forward, bringing a small chest of goods.

"This will be your disguise. It's winter, and the harsh weather has made many desperate. It doesn't help that the king has been lax about patrolling the country to hunt down robbers and the like. Petty squabbles between barons and minor lords are still common too. To protect yourselves you will wear these, and if anyone asks, you are novices who have taken the veil."

He held out two long black wimples and veils.

Mary scrunched her nose at the sight of them. A refusal looked to be forthcoming but Edith squeezed her hand to silence her.

"The journey will be hard and we might not always have the luxury of staying at a noble house," Lord Edgar Atheling said. His tone of voice left no room for argument.

Edith stepped forward to claim hers. Her lips were pressed tightly together as she helped secure it to Mary's head.

"You are brave. All of you," Lord Edgar Atheling said, looking from his namesake to the rest of them. "God be with us on our journey. We will depart in ten minutes."

"But Lord Uncle, where are you taking us? Will we live at one of your houses in England?" Edith asked.

"No, I'm afraid the small house I keep cannot accommodate you all. I have made arrangements with the King of England. Both Edgar and Alexander shall have places in his household. David, you shall continue your education and martial training with the very best. As for you girls, I am sorry, but the best place for you is with your aunt Cristina."

Edith's resolve to leave Scotland wavered at the news. Hadn't she said she would be happy to make any sacrifice if they could all be safe just a few days ago? She had to steel herself and accept her fate.

"I am sure it will all be temporary," Edgar Atheling said. "If things were different—" He clapped his hands together.

He wasn't the sort to dawdle. Like their father, he was a man of action, but he had an even temper like his sister Margaret.

Now as he gave last minute orders to his men to prepare for the journey, his steadiness assured Edith that they were doing the right thing.

SEVEN

E dith quickly discovered the nun's attire had the added benefit of providing protection against the weather storming outside. The wind buffeted their faces, while the snow and pellets of ice in the air whipped at exposed flesh as sharp as shards of glass.

They were helped onto horses and set out in the darkness shortly after they had arrived.

Edith wasn't sure how Edgar Atheling knew his way so well, but as she looked over her shoulder to watch Edinburgh disappear off in the distance, she saw that the wind and snow were already hiding their tracks. It would be hard for their uncle Donald to follow them now.

They reached the border by dawn.

"We've crossed over into England," Edgar Atheling called out to them.

"We are safe!" David cried out with joy.

Their older brothers looked triumphant too, but there was a grimness to their smiles. Perhaps they too were thinking of their future. Would they be beggars at the

English court? Edith forced back her concerns. They would make their way in the world and she believed God would right this wrong.

Now they slowed their pace stopping occasionally to rest among a copse of trees, and once they begged shelter at the barn of another abbey. But they never stayed longer than a few hours.

After days on the road, having changed horses a few times and slept in all manner of places from noble houses to peasant cottages and inns where the floor was nothing more than packed mud, the party neared the abbey. The treasure Edith had collected had been spent. Not only was she now penniless, but her clothes were caked in mud as though she were a beggar. She fretted over her appearance not out of vanity or pride but rather because of the woman she was to be reunited with.

For every family member who cared and loved her deeply there was another who was more interested in tearing her down.

Edith and her aunt Cristina had never seen eye to eye. They had spent five long years butting heads to the point where her father had been forced to intervene.

Now her father was dead and she was to be returned to her keeping. She loathed to think what retribution her aunt would exact upon her. She touched the veil she wore upon her head and wondered if she had time to cast it aside. Oh how they had fought over this scrap of material.

Her aunt had been insistent that Edith take the veil and become a nun. Again her parents had intervened. Now who would do so?

During their time together Edith had not said a word to

her uncle. She was terrified that perhaps he might see it as a good idea. The thought of living the rest of her days shut in a cloister terrified her.

But still this was better. Better than what had awaited her in Scotland. She only wished that her uncle had found her a position at the English court, but for now that was impossible. The king was still unmarried and there was no queen she might serve.

"What troubles you?" Edgar rode up beside her.

She looked at her brother, surprised he had noticed. They had never been close, but the last few months had made them rely on each other. She might even consider them to be friends.

"I don't wish to be a nun." She whispered this confession. "Not that I am ungrateful for our aunt taking us in," she added piously, as though Cristina might catch a whiff of ingratitude even from six miles away.

Edgar's eyebrow shot up. "You? A nun?" He grinned. "I can't imagine it, but I could see you as an abbess. You certainly enjoy ordering everyone around. I don't think you'd make a good nun."

"You say that as though it were a compliment. Should we not long to serve God?"

He cocked his head to the side as though she had just proved his point. "You also enjoy debating with your betters too much. You'd make a terrible novice."

Edith laughed at last. "And you give up too easily."

"When it comes to sparring with words? Yes. I confess I do. I have other tools I prefer using," he said, placing a hand on the hilt of his sword.

Edith scoffed. "Liar. You might have some skill with a

blade, but you aren't some bloodthirsty fool looking for a fight."

Edgar's expression turned grim. Perhaps he was thinking of the time Donald had stormed Edinburgh Castle. Had that only been three months ago? Time was passing by too fast for her.

A thought struck her again. "You will visit us here, won't you? I hate to think you've abandoned your sisters and flown off to have adventures at the English court."

"I promise I will visit. At the very least I'll send you long letters describing everything I've seen from the clothes to the tapestries to every morsel of food."

"Edgar, are you teasing your sister?"

Edgar jolted at the sound of their uncle riding up beside them. Edith smiled at him.

"Don't worry, Edith. I, at least, will visit as often as I can. I often have business that takes me around the country."

"Thank you, Uncle. You've been most kind and generous. I don't know how we shall ever repay you."

He tilted his head to acknowledge her words.

"I'm sure in years to come there will be plenty of ways. But I haven't acted out of purely selfish reasons. You are all my kin and I wouldn't abandon you to the wolves. In this day and age, many forget they are human and beholden to more than just their greed. Many have become little better than animals." His gaze looked distant. Then he shook himself out of whatever troubles clouded his mind. "I wrote to your aunt before I set off on my mission and I have also sent her another letter when we rested in York. She will be expecting you."

Edith nodded but couldn't quite meet his eye.

Both her uncle and older brother rode on ahead, leaving her to her gloomy thoughts. Mary and David rode in a small cart farther back. Both of them had grown tired and David was recovering from a cold. Mary's eyes caught hers and in that one look, Edith knew that she too was worried about what awaited them.

They came to the small town that lay north of the abbey. Already Edith could make out the towers of the church with its slate roof.

She'd learned long ago the history of the church. It'd been endowed for a Saxon princess before the arrival of William the Conqueror and his armies. With such a prestigious benefactress, the abbey had flourished and in time developed a reputation as a place of great learning. She and her sister had not been the only noble children learning at the abbey. Many wished to send their children here.

Up ahead, Edgar Atheling instructed one of his servants to ride out ahead to warn the abbess of their arrival.

If anything, Edith wished to slow her pace or find some excuse to avoid the reunion that was to take place.

The cobbled road led to the main entrance of the church. It was hard not to be impressed by its beauty. Travelers were welcomed by a wood carving of a life-sized Christ with his hands outstretched in welcome. Even after all these years the oak was polished and cared for so it looked like new. To the right, a candle burned in a protected recess, acting as a beacon to travelers.

Edith's eyes slid over this magnificent sight to the stone archway. The double doors were open and from the dark interior of the church her aunt emerged.

The gold pectoral cross that hung from her neck marked her out as the abbess. It gleamed against her black tunic. The oil lamp she held in one hand illuminated her severe expression. Cristina came to a stop at the threshold of the church, waiting for them to approach.

Edith thought she looked more like the angel of judgment than a saintly abbess.

If Edgar Atheling noticed this austere woman's coldness, he said nothing. Merely leaped from his horse, still agile at his age, and bowed to her.

Edith was helped down from her horse and Mary from the cart. Their meager possessions were removed from the cart.

Edith and Mary approached, huddled together, their eyes demurely downcast, and they curtsied in greeting to their aunt.

"We meet again, nieces," she said, her expression pinched. "And here you thought never to see me again."

Their uncle broke the silence. "I'm afraid they didn't bring much with them, but I'm sure you will ensure they have all that they could need." Then he gave them a sidelong look. "As princesses of Scotland."

Cristina's mouth pinched even more. She was an abbess, by now unused to being ordered about by men, especially ones who came requesting her assistance.

Edgar Atheling tried a smile. "They've been through a lot. These girls proved their mettle. You must forgive their dirty clothes. We've traveled fast and over treacherous terrain."

Cristina wasn't impressed. "You wouldn't be able to tell if there was an inch of royal blood in them. They are in rags. They come to my door as peasants."

Edith heard Edgar's sharp intake of breath.

"My lady." Now when he spoke he was stern. "These are not only your nieces but princesses. The King of England himself has promised they would receive sanctuary in his kingdom."

"And has he also vouched to pay their expenses?" Cristina retorted.

Edith knew her aunt drove a hard bargain.

"That will be managed."

It wasn't the answer Cristina was looking for and she didn't step aside to invite them in.

"Of course, if they agree to take the veil—"

"The king does not wish them to do so."

Edith looked from her aunt to her uncle. She wondered if he was lying, but she doubted he would. What was more interesting to her was the fact that the king appeared to be so interested in them at all.

"Ah." Cristina's eyes sparked with some understanding Edith hadn't quite caught on to yet. "So you've brought them here to be bargaining chips. Correct me if I am mistaken, but as far as I understand it, I am being given the honor of taking on the costs of raising these girls while you and the king are left to reap the rewards."

Any humor drained from her uncle's face. Edith hoped that he would whisk them away from here. But where could he take them even if he was so inclined?

"I will pay for their upkeep myself. But if I find anything in their education or comfort has been lacking, then you will answer not only to me but the king as well."

Cristina smiled ruefully, as though she didn't think much of his threats. "Very well. But if they wish to take holy vows, then I cannot prevent them. Even the king cannot force a maiden to relinquish her holy vows. It's the law."

Edgar Atheling sucked in his cheeks. His gaze flicked to Edith and Mary. Edith hoped he could see how much this was the last thing she would want to do.

"Of course. But only if they wish to. Without any coercion. I have already told my niece I will be visiting often and will ensure they are well treated."

Cristina let out a peal of laughter. "You make it sound as though we resort to torture." She shook her head. "You may find this hard to believe, but many women prefer the safety of this sacred life. Many long for the opportunity to escape the drudgery of everyday life and seek to devote themselves to spiritual work."

"I am surprised that you don't have a line of women pounding on your doors," he said, making a show of looking around for these supposed women desperate to be inside the abbey walls.

A muscle in Cristina's cheek twitched, but otherwise she maintained her composure.

"I apologize. That was uncalled for. For the sake of the princesses, let us put aside our amity and embrace each other like loving Christians should," Edgar Atheling said, stretching out his hands to her.

Cristina balked but, realizing she was verging on being rude, beckoned them inside, but not before she said, "Their brothers may enter but the rest of your men will stay outside."

"Is there an inn where they might rest?"

"I am sure you won't be staying long. My nieces will want to bathe and change out of such clothes—" It was then she looked at Edith and Mary. Really looked. Her brow arched. "Veils? And you say they aren't to take holy vows?"

"A necessity given our long journey," Edgar growled. "It's a common enough practice."

"What would their father say if he saw them now?" Cristina asked mockingly. She already knew the answer.

Edith looked away, ashamed of the memory. When her father had visited she'd fallen before him saying that Cristina had forced her to wear the veil and was demanding she become a nun. That wasn't so much a lie as an exaggeration.

Her father, who had been coming to discuss the potential for an alliance of marriage between a French lord and her, had been horrified.

He ripped the veil from her head and said, "You were meant to educate them to be great ladies, not to turn them into nuns." His angry words were seared into Edith's memory.

Her uncle spoke again and Edith was brought back to the present.

"Unfortunately, he is not here to offer his opinion." Edgar Atheling sighed, tiring of this exchange as they walked through the abbey. "I pray he will forgive me and understand that I am trying to do my best for his daughters."

The interior of the abbey was much as it had always been. The walls were a stony gray that sucked the light. It was a dreary place though it was well endowed and received pilgrims every year.

On the short walk to the receiving hall, Edgar Atheling had found his composure and managed to smile at them.

"You will be well taken care of here. I promise that you will come to no harm now that you are in England." Tactfully, he ignored Cristina's scoff.

Edith curtsied. "Thank you, Uncle."

Mary merely bowed her head, twisting the ends of her cloak. She had begged to be taken to see the English court, but he had refused her.

"David, Alexander, Edgar, bid farewell to your sisters," Edgar Atheling said, stepping aside.

Her eldest brother looked upon her, amused. "I had no idea there was so much bad blood between you and our aunt," he whispered. "When I pay you a visit you must tell me everything. I'd love a good laugh."

Edith grinned. "And I wish to hear your new from the court."

David stepped forward then and hugged her around the middle. She was still a head taller than him, but he was a brawny boy and she nearly toppled over.

"Be good and make sure you listen to your uncle and your older brothers."

"I promise," he said.

Then it was time for them to be off.

Edith watched the remnants of her family leave with a heavy heart. She even strained her ears to listen for their footsteps.

A heavy sigh reminded her she was now under the guardianship of their aunt.

"Well, let's get you washed and changed into something more befitting young princesses."

Mary scratched at her sleeve and Cristina flinched. "You are both likely riddled with fleas and who knows what else. We will have to burn the clothes you are wearing. Yes, Edith, even the veils."

With that, she spun on her heels and began marching away. She didn't ask them to follow her. She merely expected it. That was how their aunt was. Sharing a look with each other, Edith and Mary started after her.

"You will have your old room in the cloisters. We've had new novices join and there's no other place to put you," Cristina said, looking over her shoulder. "Though perhaps your stay here will be short."

Edith said nothing to this.

They walked through the refectory to the inner court-yard and the dormitories beyond. Beauty could still be found in the austere abbey. Apple trees had been planted in the courtyard that filled the air with their sweet scent every spring when they blossomed. Beyond the building of the abbey itself, there were several acres of farmland and pastures for grazing sheep. The wool the abbey produced was highly prized for its impeccable quality. This was wool that Edith had helped to weave into cloth herself. She had carded the strands for hours before working the strands into thick strands of string with a spindle and distaff. Her hands ached already.

They passed into the dormitories, where they ran into a few nuns returning to their rooms after a long day at work and prayer.

They bowed their heads respectfully to Cristina and

stepped aside to allow them to go past. Beyond a curious look or two, many pretended that Edith and Mary were not there.

Looking down at her clothes, Edith wondered if they assumed they were ruffians from the street. Cristina wasn't known for her generosity, but even she couldn't turn away such pitiful creatures.

"Here we are," Cristina said, opening one of the doors. The room inside was drab, but there were two cots full of furs and, best of all, a wooden tub had already been brought in. Despite her haggling with her brother, she had been prepared to take them in all along. Had she merely wanted to make them feel unwanted? Edith pushed away the uncharitable thought.

"Wash yourselves, and I'll have someone come bring you something to change into," Cristina said.

"Thank you, Aunt," Edith began, keeping her voice soft and conciliatory. "Our uncle was not exaggerating when he said we came with nothing. We don't even have a comb for our hair."

Their aunt clicked her tongue disapprovingly against the roof of her mouth. "I shall send you everything you might require. This is what happens when you leave men in charge of things. The nerve of him, dragging you two girls around like this." Then she shook her head and turned away from them without another word.

"That was peculiar," Mary said in a low voice.

"Hush, lest she hear you and change her mind." Edith pulled her inside.

A maid arrived shortly after, carrying a basket of items for them to use and, most importantly, fresh gowns.

"This is hardly what I'd consider appropriate for princesses," Mary joked as she held up one of the home-spun wool dresses dyed a shabby mahogany brown. The other was a stormy gray color. Neither was decorated with any embroidery or embellishment.

"No, but we can make do. Besides, with a bit of thread, I could transform these gowns into something you'd be proud of wearing."

Mary looked skeptical but shrugged. "Anything's better than the rags we arrived in."

"They weren't rags when we set out."

Mary laughed. "Always the contrarian." Then her expression turned somber. "Do you think our uncle will forget about us?"

"No, he promised to visit, and he isn't the sort to make empty promises."

"And Scotland? What will happen there? Will Fiona be blamed for us escaping?"

Edith bit her lip. She hadn't thought of that. Surprised at her own selfishness, it took her a long time before she gathered herself enough to reply.

"I don't believe so," she said, knowing how uncon-vincing she sounded. "There was another witness in the room. Though if they had any sense, they might have disap-peared from the castle too. We couldn't risk telling her our plans and we weren't allowed to bring anyone else with us..."

Mary patted her hand. "I'm sorry. I didn't mean to distress you. What's important is that we got away. I'm sure our uncle Donald is too busy searching for Duncan to bother with a maid who could only be accused of negligence. When he discovers we have fled to England, I doubt he will ever think about us again."

"Why not?" Edith frowned.

"We are nothing here," Mary said with a shrug. Evidently, she'd put off any thoughts of importance and grandeur far faster than Edith. "You heard our aunt. We are little better than beggars at her door. Only our noble blood sets us apart."

"Yet she doesn't take pity on us. Even though she is our aunt by blood."

Mary smiled sheepishly. "You forget her bloodline is by far superior to ours. She is from an ancient Saxon royal bloodline that ruled this land for centuries. Our lineage isn't so pure. I'm sure she believes our mother chose her husband poorly."

Edith put a hand over her mouth to hide a laugh. "You'd think a Scottish king was good enough for her."

"Ah, but he favors the Normans. The greatest sin of all," Mary said, mimicking their aunt's mannerism and voice.

"Shh. You'll get us in trouble," Edith said, her mood lighter now though.

"I wish the king was willing to do more for us than simply extending his protection." Mary sighed. "If he had adopted us..."

Edith shook her head. "That would never have happened. We are not valuable wards to hold on to. We have neither riches nor lands unless something changes. For now, we shall have to forge ahead."

PART TWO
1095

EIGHT

Edith struggled to read the book before her. The pages were crumpled and on the verge of disintegrating before her very eyes. She was seated in the scriptorium among the other nuns working on copying out manuscripts.

This particular one was written in Greek and it had not been well cared for. Her aunt had purchased it from a traveling merchant, believing that the rare volume would add to the prestige of her library.

Now it was Edith's task to copy out every word on vellum to be bound into a fresh volume. Once she was done, she would begin work on another copy. Her aunt wished to present this to the king as a present for Christmas, hoping such a magnificent gift might earn his patronage.

But Edith knew she was bound to be disappointed.

From what she had garnered from snippets of news from her uncle, he was the sort of king who preferred hunting and carousing with his courtiers to studying. While he was no longer a young man, he'd shown no interest in settling down and governing his kingdom was more of an afterthought.

Edith didn't understand why Cristina courted the king's favor. The abbey was not short on funds.

There was an abundance of noble children who'd been sent here to study, with their parents paying heavily for the honor. Beyond that, there were the pilgrims who came from far and wide. They were drawn to the holy relic—a fragment of Mary's slipper—that was on display in its own special chamber. For a small donation, they were allowed to pray before it and receive special blessings from the nuns. Miracles were known to have occurred after such pious devotion.

There were just some things she'd never understand but despite the arduous task she was given, she was grateful. It'd been three years since they fled Scotland and Edith was nearing the age most women were married by.

Most of her day was spent at study, whether that was French, Latin, and lately, Greek or arithmetic. There was always something new to learn. When she wasn't studying, she worked with the women to weave magnificent tapestries that were then sold to great households across the land. Her skill with the needle earned her the honor of adding the finishing touches to pieces with gold thread. She loved the shimmering effect it added, creating depth and drawing the eye when the light hit it.

Of course, life at the abbey could be dull, but being unencumbered by the responsibilities of being a wife meant there were certain freedoms she could enjoy.

The news from Scotland was often muddled. Only months after they had fled, their uncle Donald died in a great battle against Duncan. He now sat on the Scottish throne with Edmund as his ever-loyal companion. Yet even though he had reigned for over a year, there was still disquiet among the people.

Hearing hurried footsteps approaching, Edith put away her daydreaming and bent over her work again. She glanced up to see a novice entering the scriptorium.

Catching Edith's eye, she made a beeline for her. Then, remembering to bow, she said, "Princess Edith, you have visitors."

Visitors meant only one thing. Her uncle had come. She looked down at the drab dress she was wearing and frowned. But there was no time to change into something nicer. She stood and stretched, realizing how cramped her hand was from the painstakingly slow calligraphy work.

"Are they in the garden?" she asked the novice.

"With the abbess in her chambers."

Edith was surprised. By now her uncle had developed the careful habit of avoiding any interaction with Cristina.

"Very well, I shall go straight away."

The novice, having completed her task, disappeared.

Edith smoothed out her skirts and rearranged the girdle that hung from her waist. She smoothed a hand over her hair and ensured that no strands had escaped her braids during her morning.

During her time in the monastery she'd grown lax about her appearance. With only women allowed in the nunnery and all of them wearing a variation of the same plain habit of a nun, there was no use for vanity.

She made her way across the inner courtyard on the pebble path to the abbess's home. These accommodations gave her aunt an enviable amount of privacy. They were also used to entertain visiting dignitaries.

The door was closed, so Edith rapped and waited to be admitted.

A maid opened the door and Edith blinked as she stepped inside the darkened room.

Cristina was sitting in a high-backed chair facing the door. Her lips were pursed into a thin line of displeasure. For a moment Edith wondered if she was about to receive a lecture.

"And here she is, the Princess Edith," Cristina said.

It was then Edith noted the man sitting half covered by darkness. It was not her uncle, but a stranger she had never met before.

Her eyes flicked to her aunt for some explanation, but none was forthcoming.

The man stood. Edith grimaced as she noted his rounded belly and the wrinkles that marred his features. He was dressed in decadent silks and wore jewels on every finger. When she caught sight of the ostrich feather pinned to his hat, she had to bite back a smile. She wasn't sure who this was, but he was certainly wealthy.

Despite being an impoverished princess, Edith was still cautious of her own dignity. She waited for him to introduce himself, maintaining her regal posture.

A smile broke over his features and she saw with some horror that he was missing one of his front teeth.

"Princess, I am Alan, Duke of Bretagne." He paused for dramatic effect as he bowed to her with a little flourish. "I have come from the court of King William Rufus, with letters of introduction."

"It is a pleasure to meet you, Your Grace," Edith said, offering him a shallow curtsy, deep enough not to be rude but not overly respectful either.

"The king has told me of your great beauty and I see that he has not exaggerated."

Edith didn't blink or look away as he studied her. Inwardly, she cringed at his crudeness. How would the king know what she looked like? The king had never seen her in person.

"Your uncle has told me you've been entrusted to the care of your aunt and are quite a devout lady. I see that must indeed be true for you are dressed more like a peasant than a princess," he said, letting out a loud guffaw as if he had not just insulted her. "That is all well and good. I cannot abide women who are vain and care for nothing but rich clothes. Not that my coffers couldn't bear such an expense."

Edith caught that and, for the first time in years, felt a sliver of fear wind its way through her. She remained silent in the face of such indignation, so it was Cristina who interjected.

"We lead a quiet life here. Our devotion to God comes before all else," Cristina said.

"Good. Good. But I hope you aren't so inclined to the religious life?" Duke Alan asked.

Edith didn't reply, but neither did she deny it.

"As per the king's wishes she has not taken vows. Yet," Cristina said.

"There's a pleasant river that runs near the abbey. Would I be overstepping the mark if I asked the princess to accompany me?" he asked. A challenge flashed across his features and for a moment Edith wondered if her aunt would dare refuse him. She certainly looked like she wished for nothing more than to have this duke thrown out of her abbey, if only for his insolence.

"I will come and act as a chaperone."

"Certainly. The more the merrier," Duke Alan said, clapping his hand on his belly. "And perhaps after I might sample that famous honeyed ale Romsey is renowned for."

"We are renowned for many things," Edith said, finding her voice at last. "Perhaps you should like to see our collection of manuscripts and the illumination work the nuns here do. I, myself, am working on a Greek translation."

"Are you indeed?" His brow arched. "Literate, eh?"

"I can speak three languages and write fluently in two of them."

"Excellent," he said, but his expression didn't match the exuberance in his tone. Without further delay, he offered her his arm and, not wishing to be impolite, she took it. Cristina held the door open for them and this time allowed them to take precedence.

Edith wondered at her mask of indifference. What was her aunt thinking? And more importantly, what was going on? She wasn't such an ingénue without knowledge of the world, but surely the king wouldn't ask her to marry this man. He was more than twice her age. Her uncle would intercede on her behalf. Surely. Yet for all his assurances that he had her best interest in mind, doubt gnawed at her.

It was late spring, and the ground beneath the apple trees was littered with a blanket of snowy white petals.

Edith wished she could sit among them, breathing in the sweet scent. Sadly, they continued on their way through the inner courtyard and out the gates to the land beyond.

Surrounding Romsey were several acres of arable land. A river cut through the fields separating the abbey from the monastic farming land that kept them all fed.

"Such a pretty little convent," Duke Alan commented as he glanced around.

Edith bit her tongue to keep from correcting him. She didn't wish to be accused of being rude. He was a duke after all, and if he held the favor of the king then she ought to tread carefully.

He didn't wait for her to comment but went on to describe a church he had founded. It was in every way superior to Romsey.

Edith distracted herself by admiring the peaceful landscape before them.

Indeed, at the moment Romsey looked idyllic. A beekeeper was tending to the hive, and the grass was an emerald green. In the pasture beyond the river, fat white sheep dotted the landscape. In the herb garden, nuns moved around caring for the plants and tilling the soil.

"We're reaching one of the many fish ponds," Edith said, speaking without intending to. "We keep eels in one and trout in another. It is best they are kept separate so they don't eat each other. Our abbey is known for its fresh fish and grilled eel. We don't need to buy any fish at the market."

"Ah," Duke Alan said, his eyes twinkling with amusement. She supposed that as a duke, where his fish came from didn't interest him. "You have a very industrious mind. Perfect for a Chatelain."

They'd come to it at last. Edith's mouth went dry and she struggled to keep her composure.

"I was encouraged from birth to learn all I could," she said.

"Indeed. And can you ride? Hawk? Play the harp?"

She nodded and was rewarded with a pat on her hand. Edith flinched at the touch.

"When you are no longer living so strictly,"—Duke Alan winked at her—"you will enjoy such luxuries again."

Edith gave no reply and they walked on for quite a while.

"You must be aware, my lady, that the king may grant your hand in marriage to one of his vassals."

Turning her head so he would not see the way her mouth twisted with disgust, she nodded.

"Some have made inquiries, but none have put forward their suit." He paused, hoping to build anticipation. "Except me."

Edith was aghast. Did he really think such words would flatter her? Was she to think herself truly so pathetic she should feel grateful to him for his offer?

"I was intrigued by your lineage. Indeed, the story of your parents has become something of folklore around the court. I met her once, you know. Your mother was a beautiful lady."

Edith swallowed hard. Her mother had last been at the English court some twenty years ago. That all but confirmed his age. He took her continued silence as an invitation to go on disparaging her.

"I am not ashamed to admit I am a wealthy man. So I have the privilege of choosing any bride that takes my fancy. I know you may never receive a proper dowry. I am aware the situation in Scotland is tenuous at best and you didn't leave on the best terms with your half-brother. But fear not. The king has assured me you would not come to me as a pauper. Not that I care."

Edith remained mute with indignation. This man couldn't be serious. She had never met such a ridiculous person before. But she could see that far from being the foolish man he appeared, he had a very specific strategy in mind. By throwing his insults around so freely he belittled her and made her feel as though she had no other option but to marry him and be damn grateful for the chance. If Edith had been weaker or less confident, she might have leaped at his offer. But she knew even without a dowry, her royal lineage was far more valuable.

"I would like to hear your answer before I return to court. The king is anxious for my company." There was an unmistakable edge of pride in his voice as he said this.

But Edith wondered if the king truly valued him or if he merely valued all that gold the duke possessed.

Ignoring him completely, Edith turned the topic to something else entirely. "What of Jerusalem, my lord? Are you not keen to go yourself? All the greatest men in Christendom are flocking to the Pope's standard. I have heard the French king plans to go."

His brows furrowed at this question. "The Holy War? Why, no. I mean, certainly I have donated handsomely to the cause. As has the English king. But I have no plans to go myself."

"Why?" The question was innocent enough and she had given him no cause to suspect her of teasing him, yet he still spluttered over a reply.

"Well, Princess Edith, it is not as simple as that. I have

responsibilities. Grave ones. I don't have the luxury of leaving my lands unattended. There is the matter of my marriage as well."

She hummed in understanding.

"My lord, this is all I have." She pulled away and, with a wave of her hand, pointed to her simple gown. "I am not worthy of such an honor you seek to bestow on me. Surely there are eligible ladies far better suited to your needs. I have lived a cloistered life away from the pomp and ceremony of court. While I play the harp, I do not dance. Nor could I claim to have a merry disposition."

He hesitated but after some consideration smiled. "As I have said, I know of your shortcomings. The rest I am sure you will learn in due time. I am patient. All I expect is for a wife to be obedient."

Subservient, Edith thought bitterly. She tried again, daring to look at her aunt, who was standing off to the side doing her best to appear as though she was not listening to the whole debacle. Edith could see that there would be no help from that quarter.

"Your Grace, I must be frank with you. I find myself at peace when I am here with these great ladies, praying devoutly before the altar of Our Lord. There is no greater solace to me than this." She hung her head down low for good measure.

Duke Alan took a step back. "You wish to take the veil?"

"I am a devout woman," Edith said, sidestepping the question. She'd become quite adept at doing so. When she looked up, she thought she could see the corner of her aunt's lips curl up in mirth.

The duke looked at Cristina, who was no help in this matter.

"I have done my duty as required by the king. She has not taken the veil, and certainly I will not force her to do so. Yet I also cannot prevent her should she wish to. It is my duty as abbess."

Duke Alan sputtered at this. He glanced around as though wishing to find support hidden in the foliage. "The king—he told me. You should be honored." He gave Edith a look full of accusation. "You should be grateful."

"Oh, I am," Edith rushed to say. "Yet it doesn't change my inclination. Nor do I feel I am worthy of such an honor."

"I will speak to the king," he said, sounding more like a disappointed child than a duke now. "He will make you see sense. I bid you farewell." He nodded his head toward her. Then, turning to the abbess, he bowed more respectfully but stormed off nonetheless.

The two women watched him stomp back toward the entrance of the abbey, where his men waited on horseback. They hadn't even bothered dismounting. Clearly, he'd come here expecting to conclude the business quickly.

"Well." Cristina clapped her hands together. "As much as I loathe interruptions, I found that amusing."

"Aunt, what will happen? Will I be forced to marry him?" Edith's bravery wavered.

Her aunt paused mid-step. "It will not be the last we about it. He may have been the first in a long line of suitors. There is something you can do to save yourself from marriage to a Norman."

"What?"

"Take the veil. Swear on the Bible that you wish to

relinquish all earthly goods and take the veil. The king will not be able to force you to marry against your wishes then. I can write to the Archbishop of Canterbury and ask him to support me in this—"

Edith lowered her eyes, her mouth set in a grim line of determination.

Her aunt scoffed. "That old stubbornness again. What do you want out of life? You won't be able to go on denying every suitor that comes calling now that you are of an age to be married. You cannot have the freedom and peace of the cloister without committing yourself." Her cheeks grew red with rage and Edith flinched. "You should be grateful for everything you have." She stopped in her tirade to cough. It racked her body so much that she shook, and Edith stepped forward to steady her, only to be pushed away again.

"Stubborn girl, go pray for forgiveness and see to your work. I won't always be here to protect you."

"I don't recall you ever protecting me," Edith said.

Her aunt slapped her with enough force that her head flew to one side. Edith touched her cheek, feeling the heat of her skin. She'd gone too far. It was the outburst of a child and somewhat untrue. Her aunt could've forced her to accept Duke Alan's suit. She could have even summoned a priest to make the engagement binding. Watching her aunt storm off, she regretted her words.

Sighing, she went in search of her sister to tell her the news.

NINE

"Tell me again," Mary said with a laugh.

"I don't want to repeat it for a third time." Edith kicked at a loose stone in their path. "He told me outright that I should be glad anyone wished to marry me at all and that I should be grateful to him for even asking me."

"I suppose he wanted you to kiss his boot as well," Mary scoffed.

"One would never guess you were raised in a convent," Edith said, side-eyeing her sister.

"That is something I'm very proud of." Mary grinned and leaped on ahead. "I hate it here. There's nothing to do."

"There's plenty. It's just you'd prefer to gossip or dance the day away."

"Exactly. That's my problem. I don't get to do any of that." She sighed wistfully. "I hope next Christmas Uncle will take us with him to court and let us celebrate with him."

"We were quite merry here last year."

Mary stopped mid-stride and studied her sister carefully.

"You are as shy as a deer. When have you ever been so eager to remain at Romsey?"

Edith shrugged. She'd been mulling over the interaction with Duke Alan and what it meant for her. "I thought we'd been forgotten. Tucked away here in this little place. But it is clear I was wrong, and I fear now that the door has been opened it shall never be closed again. I don't wish to be a nun, especially one under our aunt's thumb. But neither do I wish to be shackled in marriage to an oaf like that duke."

Mary held her hands and squeezed lightly. "I am sorry. At the very least, we shall have to make sure you don't get sent off to some dreary place like Bretagne."

"You've never been to Bretagne. How do you know what it is like? I have it on very good authority that it's a wonderful place."

They rounded the bend in the garden approaching the limestone walls of the abbey chancellery where they could see the large arched windows. Edith came to a stop and held her sister's hand.

"We shall be free one day. Not beholden to anyone."

Mary was far more skeptical than she was. It was surprising that out of the two of them she was the more cynical one.

"You still believe in Edgar's dreams?"

"There's a real chance. The king is eager to support his claim to Scotland. Think of that."

"I would rather not return, and even if we did, what would await us? Edgar might be fond of us, but he won't let us be his spinster sisters forever."

"He must not love us very much then," Edith chuckled.

Then, knowing she must put aside all her childish fears and anxieties, she straightened her shoulders and held her head up straight.

"We must not fear. *Deus lo volt!*" God wills it. The battle cry of the Crusade.

Weeks later, while working with Sister Alice in the kitchens making jam, Edith was once again interrupted by the arrival of visitors. She was wearing her hair tied back with a scarf and froze the moment someone came to fetch her.

Before anyone could stop her, she fled to her room. She hastily tied on a wimple and veil she'd borrowed from a novice. If another suitor had come to call, then she would to go on pretending she intended to say her vows.

She ran into her aunt Cristina, who looked her up and down with contempt. "They're down by the stables."

Edith's eyes lit up. Her uncle or her brother had come.

She took off at a run, excitement overcoming any sense of decorum.

She only stopped when she neared the stables. A little breathless, she spotted her uncle and called out to him.

"My lord uncle!"

He turned toward her, but Edith could see the smile melt from his features the moment he saw her.

She ran toward him, curtsying. "Dearest uncle, I hope all is well with you. Whatever is the matter?"

"I have heard distressing rumors and I see now that they are true. You've been called to the religious life."

ANNE R BAILEY

It was then that Edith remembered she was wearing a
makeshift veil. Flushing, she pulled at the material, not
caring it left her hair in disarray.

"You are mistaken," she said. "It is nothing more than a
deception. I'm sure you've heard the Duke of Bretagne
wished to marry me. Just a few days after his visit, he sent a
messenger with a little gift for me. When I greeted him, I
donned a veil. I have heard nothing about it since."

"And you never will," said a strange voice to her left,
followed by a snort of amusement that had her whipping
around.

She was taken aback to find a stranger, maybe a few
years older than herself, standing there. He was of medium
build with dark hair and eyes. But there was something
about the way he carried himself and the half smile on his
face that caught her attention.

Suddenly, feeling self-conscious, she smoothed down
her hair.

"Niece, may I introduce you to Prince Henry," Edgar
Atheling said.

"I—I, Your Grace." Edith bobbed up and down, at a loss
for words. Her face felt hot with embarrassment. This was
certainly no way to meet a prince. Especially not the
brother of the king who held her life in his hands.

"My lady, it is good to finally meet you. I've heard a lot
about you."

Edith wasn't sure if that was meant as a compliment
or not.

"I must apologize."

"For?" He cocked his head to the side.

116

She flushed anew but didn't look away. "My deception." She held up her veil.

He fixed her with a look she couldn't discern.

"As Prince Henry said, you needn't worry yourself about Lord Alan anymore," her uncle said.

"Why not? Has he found another bride?"

"He has died of the flux."

"Ah. I am so sorry to hear that. I shall pray for his soul."

Prince Henry caught her eye again. "Pray for his soul if you feel you need to, but you needn't pay lip service to him because I am here."

He had guessed her intention so easily that Edith was struck mute for a moment. Then, sheepish, she said, "Maybe I am not exactly sorry that I have escaped his attentions. However, I didn't wish him to come to any harm either."

"That is commendable of you."

Edgar Atheling interrupted them. "I am afraid my visit will be short. We are on our way to join the fight against Lord Robert Mowbray. The prince's tutor, Bishop Osmund, has traveled with us, but he has been injured and will recover here at the abbey."

Edith crossed herself. "He will receive the best care here. Aunt Cristina mentioned there was rebellion brewing in Northumberland. We all pray for the success of the king's army. May God help the rebels see the error of their ways and beg for forgiveness."

Again Henry snorted. "It will take more than prayer to bring down the rebels. Northumberland has always been a vain fool, but now he has overstepped."

"Henry," Edgar Atheling warned.

"No, uncle, I wish to know what is happening in the kingdom," Edith said.

With a shrug, Prince Henry continued, "Northumberland is claiming my father was a mere usurper and that our line is cursed. He promises that the kingdom will return to the way it was governed before Hastings. "

Edith looked at her uncle. If Prince Henry's father hadn't won the battle, then her uncle might've been king. "The crown changes hands many times. Look at Scotland. But I am surprised he has chosen now to complain."

Prince Henry looked amused.

"It's merely a pretense. Northumberland thinks my brother is weak and, indeed, the king has faced a few setbacks recently that have made him unpopular."

"But there's no doubt this rebellion will be stopped," Edgar Atheling said confidently.

Edith had been mulling over Henry's words. He hadn't said it, but it was the Saxon people who were rallying to Northumberland's side. Under Norman rule, they were second-class citizens. Life was hard under normal circumstance but they faced curfews, discrimination and heavy taxes. No wonder they were easily tempted by promises of reform. Her heart ached at the injustice, but there was nothing she could do.

"Perhaps, if your brother might reconsider his stance on the laws and taxes he's imposed upon the Saxons then they wouldn't be so easily swayed by false promises," she said, watching Prince Henry closely. Would he grow angry with her? Would he call her an ignorant fool?

He pinched the bridge of his nose. "It's a complicated matter. Old resentments still linger in the hearts of many.

And yet, I wish my brother would try to bring peace among the Normans and Saxons."

Edgar Atheling decided it was time to interject. "We must ride out at first light. Princess Edith, will you ask your aunt if there is room for us in the guesthouse? And I long for a good meal."

"I shall ask her," Edith said, eager to be of help. She was already turning to leave when her uncle called after her. "And we have much to discuss about you and your sudden eagerness for the veil."

"Yes, uncle," she said, keeping her head down, but not before Henry had caught sight of her defiant look.

Cristina sent a servant to arrange the lodgings for their distinguished guest. She made an appearance as they were settling in and greeted the young prince with a special smile and indulged his request for a private dinner. Edith knew her aunt must be wincing internally at the mounting costs of accommodating him. No doubt, she was determined to recoup the losses somehow.

"Since you desire it, we shall dine in my private chambers. I shall have a table carried in and you shall eat as befits your station," she said in a sugary tone.

Edith, who was standing off to the side, rolled her eyes. This didn't go unnoticed by Henry, who grinned at her when Cristina wasn't looking.

Apparently, despite her aunt's best efforts, Henry had sensed she disliked him and only tolerated him because he was a prince.

Edith wondered what he would say if he knew it went a lot deeper than simply disliking him. Her aunt despised the Normans, but she held a special hatred for the spawn of William the Conqueror. However, she wasn't a fool. She needed their patronage and protection. If the price of this wealth was courting their favor, then she would.

"Abbess, Lord Edgar has desired to see his nieces for many months. I don't suppose you could give me a tour of your abbey while they speak, could you?" Prince Henry asked.

"Certainly, I would be honored."

"Good, I shall see you later, Lord Edgar," he said and then offered his arm to the abbess, who looked at it as though it were a poisonous snake.

Forcing herself to smile, she led him away. "We shall begin in the church."

When they were out of earshot, Edgar Atheling turned to her. "Well, I've never seen your aunt so keen to please someone until now."

"And I doubt you ever will." Edith smiled, her eyes still fixed on where Cristina had stood a moment ago.

"Tell me, niece, why are you threatening to become a nun?"

They found a bench, listening to birdsong as the sparrows flew from tree to tree.

"Uncle, he was a horrid man. I couldn't have—I didn't wish to be married to him." Edith said this while looking down at her hands in her lap. "You didn't support the match. Did you?"

He eyed her. "He was a wealthy man. A favorite of the king."

She waited, sensing that there was more to it.

"Who you marry is up to the king. You cannot scare off all your suitors by threatening to take the veil. The king would order you to rescind your vows and marry you off anyway," he said, then let out a sigh. "But no. I couldn't have borne the thought of you marrying a man like that. He was a fool, at court and on the battlefield."

"Thank you, Uncle." Edith felt instant relief. She wished she was still a young girl and could throw her arms around him in a tight embrace.

"The king heard about this incident. Of course, he sees this as some failing in you. You will have to tread carefully with him from now on. Don't expect him to grant you any favors or special consideration in the future." Edgar shook his head sorrowfully.

"But I delayed and bought myself some time. I would've thought that was a good strategic move on my part," Edith said.

"You were lucky. What if the king forced you to marry Duke Alan? The duke wouldn't have thanked you for causing all this trouble."

"Uncle." Edith smiled. "You are intent on being upset with me and lecturing me, but I can tell your heart is not in it."

He scoffed but didn't disagree.

"Trust me to manage my affairs. I have dealt with far worse than someone like Duke Alan."

"Oh?"

"You have met my Aunt Cristina, have you not? Even he couldn't contend with her."

Edgar chuckled. "How has she been? She wrote to me in last summer that she has been unwell."

That took Edith by surprise. She was aware her aunt's cough had grown worse, but she hadn't known that it was serious enough that she would write to her brother.

"She is a hard woman, but she knows that her duty lies to God and her family," Edgar said. "Personally, I hope she recovers and is able to remain as a guardian for you and your sister."

Edith hadn't imagined that was even a possibility. Would they have to leave Romsey Abbey if she died? She couldn't see why.

"I wished to tell you that I shall be traveling and don't know when I'll be able to visit you again."

"I am sorry to hear that," Edith said with genuine sadness in her voice.

"I have reminded your brothers of their duty to look after you and Mary."

"They've certainly been lax in that quarter. David is the only one who writes regularly."

Edgar Atheling smiled. "My namesake is preoccupied riding about the country at the king's beck and call. King William Rufus certainly keeps us gainfully employed. But he also rewards those loyal to him. He has promised to fund my journey to Jerusalem."

"Yet, the king still refuses to go on Crusade?"

"Yes. Though he has promised to assist by providing funds and men whenever he can. A fleet of ships is being prepared. However, he's one of the few kings in Christendom who is not going himself. What does this say about him and the state of this country?"

He was challenging her. Her uncle always felt that studying and leading a life of solitude in the nunnery left her weak when it came to politics. But this was not the case. She considered the situation carefully. Remembering the taxes the king had enacted on his people last quarter day. She'd been impressed by Prince Henry. However, it was hard not to notice the patchwork repair on his doublet, even if it was made of rich damask wool.

"I suspect he doesn't have anyone he would trust to manage his kingdom while he is gone."

Her uncle inclined his head.

"More than that, there is also unrest in England. The lords of the land are unsettled. He's seen as an ineffectual king. They could always depose him and turn to his older brother, Robert, who is waiting across the channel. I'm sure he's eagerly waiting for the perfect opportunity to strike."

Edgar Atheling nodded. "You have the gist of it. We are being attacked on three fronts. It makes it difficult for the king to leave the nation in such a state."

"Could England even support the king on crusade? The crop yield has been weak two years in a row."

He grinned. "You would've made a good merchant. I'm sure there would be a way to find the funds. The Pope is eager to pay for this noble enterprise. Duke Robert, the king's brother, went because his nobles forced him to go."

Edith nodded. Of the three surviving sons of William the Conqueror, Robert was the eldest and had inherited Normandy. He'd quickly squandered his inheritance and was beholden to his nobles. Now he was merely a figurehead.

"What of Prince Henry? Where does he fit in all of this?"

Her uncle eyed her. "He is as sharp as a blade. As talented on the battlefield as he is debating policy with the king's councilors. I've never seen a man look at a castle and determine how to lay siege to it so quickly and efficiently. But he is a pauper, dependent on his brothers for the very clothes on his back."

So much like her. Edith looked down at her plain dress. Together with Mary, she'd stitched a pattern of dark green leaves around the neckline, but it was plain and more suitable for a nun than a princess. At least Prince Henry's brothers kept him in silks and gave him his freedom. She wasn't free to do as she pleased, but likely that had more to do with the fact she was a woman than anything else.

With a mental shake of her head she turned her attention back to her uncle. "So after you quell the rebellions in Northumberland and fight in the Crusades, where will you go?" She'd meant her question as a jest, but a fire shone in his eyes.

"To Scotland. Soon it will be time to strike."

TEN

Remembering her promise, Edith made her way the infirmary only to find Sister Mary arguing with an elderly man.

"May I be of some assistance?" Edith asked, approaching.

They both looked at her.

"Perhaps you might fetch the abbess for me, my child," the man said. "I refuse to be confined to a bed."

"You are ill and will only make yourself feel worse if you continue on like this," Sister Mary said, incredulously.

It was hard to believe that this stubborn man was Bishop Osmund, tutor and advisor to the prince.

"Why?" The question slipped out and he looked at her arching a brow. Embarrassed, she cleared her throat and said, "If you are injured, why do you refuse to rest?"

"There is nothing to do and I fear my mind would decay faster than my mortal body."

Sister Mary rolled her eyes, even Edith felt it was a rather dramatic sentence.

"What if I read to you? The abbey has an excellent library."

He looked intrigued. A fatherly smile spread across his features. "Can you read Latin?"

"Yes, and even a little Greek," she said, unable to keep her pride from her tone.

"Very well. If you shall humor an old man, I shall rest," he said, in a serious tone as though giving a solemn oath.

Sister Mary let out an relieved sigh.

As Bishop Osmund headed back to his bed, Edith noted the heavy limp in his left leg. What had possessed him to travel in this condition?

As she arranged the pillows for him she could feel him studying her.

"And who do I have to thank for rescuing me?"

"I am Edith—"

The name sparked a look of recognition in his eye. "As in the exiled Princess of Scotland?"

She bowed her head.

"I met your brothers at court. The youngest David is a spirited fellow. Very bright."

"I am happy to hear that. In Scotland, he ran from his tutors whenever he got the chance."

The Bishop guffawed. "They were likely boring him. I found he's very advanced for his age."

They settled down into a steady conversation until Sister Mary returned from her rounds and brought then a book. Edith had been reading for quite some time when Prince Henry arrived.

"I see there was no need to come entertain you," Prince Henry said, carrying a chessboard in his hands.

Bishop Osmund eyed him. "I am very well looked after by this young lady. Unlike you, she has patience to read to me. I'm sure you have other things to do."

Edith looked to the side, trying to hide a smile.

Despite the dismissal, his gaze kept drifting to the chessboard. Just as Henry appeared as though he might leave, he said, "But I have been selfish. She deserves a rest. Set up the board and I shall play with you."

"As you wish," Prince Henry said. "On the condition that when I am gone, you will listen to the advice of these godly ladies and rest. I know how stubborn you can be."

"I taught you your letters, Prince Henry. Don't think you can command me now." Bishop Osmund huffed, but in the end, relented.

Edith watched this all with barely contained amusement. She was pleasantly surprised by the care and attention Prince Henry paid his old tutor. It was clear he cared for him deeply.

"Do you play, Princess Edith?" The Bishop asked.

She nodded.

"Then perhaps, after I give this arrogant pup a good thrashing you can be my next opponent."

Edith laughed. "Very well."

It was a very close match but Prince Henry emerged the victor. Far from being disappointed, the Bishop looked pleased by his protégé. "Now you must play against the Princess."

"I don't think—" Henry began, but was interrupted by Edith.

"I'd love to." Her eyes met his, full of challenge.

In the end, they played two games with her winning the

first and him the second. Both Prince and Bishop were impressed with her skill.

"I won't deny I underestimated you, Princess," Prince Henry said, but he stopped short of issuing any other compliment.

That evening Edith and Mary ate with their uncle and Henry in their aunt's private chamber. Cristina had excused herself and so they were alone to enjoy the decadent food and rich wine of her private cellars.

"I don't know why I don't do this more often," Prince Henry said, patting his belly. "My time is wasted at court. If I simply traveled around England and allowed people to pay homage to me, I would do rather well for myself."

Edith looked at him sideways. Disgusted that he would be willing to take advantage of people like that.

"You don't because you have more sense than that," Edgar Atheling said, setting down his mug of ale.

"I've offended your niece," Henry said, leaning forward.

Edith looked away quickly. He was more attentive than he let on.

"Perhaps you should be more careful with your words," Edgar said.

Henry scoffed but turned to Edith, who was sitting at the end of the table with her sister. "I do apologize. It's often that I speak without thinking. Usually no one pays any attention to me, so I am free to say whatever comes to mind."

Edith met his gaze. "Your plan wouldn't work. After a

time, you would garner a reputation as a beggar prince and no one would welcome you into their hall."

He blinked, then leaned back in his chair and laughed. He reached for the flagon of wine and refilled his cup. "If you must know, I have already earned that moniker. Though it has little to do with my unwillingness to earn my coin but rather the pesky fact I am the youngest brother. My elder brothers inherited dukedoms and kingdoms, while I was given nothing more than a few coins." He shook his head sorrowfully. "If I had been wiser, I would've been born further up the list."

The edge of Edith's lip tugged. She was determined not to be enchanted or amused by this princeling with his debonair attitude and direct manner of speaking.

"Your uncle told me that you play the harp. Lady Mary, would you grace us with a song?"

Mary, at her side, was far more taken in by being in the presence of a prince of England. She bowed and hurried to bring her harp from their room.

Edgar Atheling shook his head. "While I am away, I shall rely on your brother Edgar to look after you. Bishop Osmund has also vouched to keep an eye out for you, and Prince Henry as well. They will speak for me while I am away. Hopefully, the king will listen to them."

Edith's brow arched incredulously. "I can look after myself."

"Yes, but you are here at Romsey. Your future isn't being decided in these hallowed halls but rather at court," Henry interjected. "I wouldn't turn away our help. With your uncle leaving, we will be your only window into the outside world. Worry not. Your brother and uncle are my close friends, and though you might dislike me, I am honor bound to serve you and your sister."

That silenced Edith. Thankfully, Mary returned. She sat before the brazier, strumming her fingers lightly over the strings to test them before leaping into a beautiful song.

The following day, Edith and Mary woke early in order to bid her uncle farewell. Before he left, he handed them the presents he'd brought; pearl pins for their hair and a bolt of cloth for new gowns. Edith wasn't sure when she'd have time to sew them, but she looked forward to seeing what she could make out of the forest green material.

As the two men rode off with their armed guard, Edith said a silent prayer for her uncle's safe return.

Two months later, the Abbess Cristina took to her sickbed. Her uncle had been right to fear for his sister's health.

All the nuns of the abbey prayed for her soul day and night. A special vigil was even held for her recovery. Edith and Mary tended to her as often as they could, but she often sent them away in favor of Alice, one of her favored sisters, to sit by her side.

The abbey was already in a state of unrest when a retinue of guards bearing the king's banner were seen riding up the road to Romsey.

"Who could it be?" Mary asked as they watched from the tower.

Edith shrugged. "Perhaps it's travelers or tax collectors. Let's go. We don't have time to dawdle." She pulled her sister along to the kitchens, where the cook was preparing a thin broth for their aunt. Edith went to a workbench and, together with Mary, began preparing a tisane of pepper- mint, thyme, and lavender to help with their aunt's cough. They'd been taught to brew this by one of the other nuns, who was renowned for her cures. This work felt more fulfilling than dabbing at their aunt's forehead with cool water.

Edith forgot about the visitors until a servant came to fetch both Edith and Mary.

"You are wanted in the church," the maid said, sniffing.

Edith and Mary set aside their aprons and went quickly to see what was the matter.

The nun who was next in command after the abbess was speaking to one of the men. Her tone was argu- mentative.

Edith drew back, and then she recognized it was Prince Henry to whom she was speaking. The other two men with him bore the livery of the king of England, but neither her uncle nor her brother were anywhere in sight.

She'd had little news from him and she prayed that Henry had not come bearing sad tidings.

With slow careful steps she approached.

They heard her approach and turned as one.

"Princess Edith." Henry greeted her with a bow and repeated the gesture to Mary.

"Prince Henry has come with instructions from the king," the nun said, holding out a letter to Edith. "You are commanded to leave Romsey Abbey and retire to Wilton Abbey to be closer to London and the court."

Edith's eyes scanned the letter, disbelief flooding her.

Her eyes snapped to Henry, who, far from looking pleased by the news, looked upset.

"The king must not know that my aunt is very ill. We cannot leave her at this critical time," Edith said, straightening her back.

Henry met her eyes and she could see from his expression that it did not matter. The king had waited a long time to exact his revenge for her disobedience. It had come now and Edith felt the full weight of his authority.

"We are here to see you escorted safely to Wilton. The king has generously provided you with horses for the journey and a cart for your things," Henry said. Then a glint of mischief entered his expression. "However, there's no need for us to leave right this moment. We can leave tomorrow."

One of the men behind him sputtered at that. "What do you mean, Prince Henry?"

Henry rounded on him. "We've spent the better part of the day riding here. I am tired and I look forward to a good meal and some rest. Besides it would be safer to travel by daylight."

The man looked at the stormy clouds outside and hesitated.

"My brother charged me with this task, Lord Humphrey, not you. But if you wish, you may complain to the king. I doubt he will care one way or another."

"And you are far too carefree in carrying out his instructions," Lord Humphrey said, but he stopped short of arguing any further.

"Since that is settled, I must pay my respects to the abbess and assure her that the king will look after her nieces," Henry said, stretching his arms overhead. "Then we should have something to eat." This last bit he spoke to the stunned nun.

"We shall ensure everything will be ready for you, my lords. The guesthouse can house everyone in your party."

Henry shrugged. "Don't trouble yourselves. They can rest in town at the inn."

The men behind him blanched. Inns were of varying qualities. But the prince was intent on exerting his power over them and commanded them to leave the abbey.

He reminded Edith of the rooster who had gotten into the hencoop and strutted around, happy for the chance to push around his weight and show them who was in charge.

The following day the heavens poured down on Romsey and Henry declared happily that the roads were terrible and that they would have to wait yet another day before setting off.

Edith found him eating in the refectory, sitting with the priest and his servants.

He excused himself and came over to speak to her.

"Milady?"

"I wanted to thank you," she said. "You gave us two more days here at Romsey."

"I have no idea what you mean. But I am flattered if you think I can command the weather."

Edith's gratitude was washed away by his infuriating dismissal. He was teasing her but it still frustrated her to no end.

"Well, you still have my thanks."

"Thank God if you must, Princess Edith. If you wish to further delay, you might consider having an accident tomorrow. A twisted ankle could leave you bedridden for a few more days. Just a thought." Henry winked and then he was off.

Edith frowned after him. He was incorrigible. If there were ever someone who was inclined to cause trouble, it was him. But she appreciated his reserve. Any other man might have been happy to claim the credit for himself and bask in the praise.

———

The following day the sky was a bright blue and there were no more excuses to delay their journey.

Edith visited her aunt in her private chambers. She approached solemnly, knowing this might be the last time she saw her, and kneeled by her bedside. The sight of her aunt's gaunt features reminded her of her mother and she immediately crossed herself.

"I expect you shall not mourn for me when I am gone. Nor would I want you to," her aunt said, laying a heavy hand on her head. "I will be with God soon enough and all my toils here on earth will come to an end."

Another cough racked her.

"Reverend Mother, you are mistaken. We may have not seen eye to eye, but I appreciate all you have done for my sister and me."

Cristina's eyes studied her face and, finding no deception in her features, dared to smile.

"I am told you are leaving me. It is unfortunate that the king should decide to take you away from me now. You will enjoy greater freedoms at Wilton Abbey, but remember not to let it go to your head. Live your life as an obedient daughter of the church and you shall be rewarded. I wish you had listened to me and taken the veil. How much longer will you be able to live a life walking on the border between two worlds?"

"I understand. But rather than squabble, I'd appreciate your blessing, Aunt Cristina." Edith bowed her head. "My sister as well."

Cristina murmured a quick prayer over her.

"We shall pray for your recovery," Mary said somberly.

"Pray that my suffering on this earth shall come to a speedy end," Cristina said, with a sardonic smile. By now she'd grown tired and her breath raspy. "Go now, and may God watch over you."

"Amen," both girls said. Still kneeling, they bowed their heads and crossed themselves. Slowly they got to their feet and exited the darkened chamber.

At the doors of the abbey gates, Henry and the armed retinue waited for them.

Their belongings were meager. The abbey had placed their worldly belongings in three chests, but they were half empty. The prioress who'd been fond of Mary let her take the harp she often played on and prepared a generous helping of preserves and pies for their journey.

"Go in peace," she told the girls.

"You will have to ride astride," Henry said, coming up to them. "Or you may ride in the cart. The choice is up to you."

"I prefer to ride," Edith said.

Mary, not to be outdone by her elder sister, agreed too.

The cloak and dress Edith wore were long and covered her legs and feet once she was up in the saddle. Riding astride was far more comfortable than using a sidesaddle, but also less dignified. It took Edith a moment to adjust to being on horseback again. It'd been over two years since she had had the luxury. But as they set off, with the guards riding ahead, she quickly settled in, enjoying the breeze on her face and the mare's steady pace.

As they traveled on the main road, those on foot stepped to the side to allow their armed retinue to ride past.

Edith couldn't help frowning when one guard, spat in the direction of a group of bedraggled travelers and muttered under his breath, "Dirty Saxon scum."

Horrified by his rudeness, she threw a coin to them. They called out blessings upon her, which only made the guard scowl.

"Don't encourage them."

Didn't he realize that both she and her sister were of Saxon descent? Maybe he didn't care.

Before Edith could think much of it, she was interrupted by Prince Henry riding up beside her.

"Is all well?"

Not wishing to cause a stir, she nodded. "I merely wished to help them."

"If you go on throwing coins, we will become targets for bandits." He must have caught her crestfallen expression because he added, "You have a generous heart not found in many."

With the cart hampering their progress the party could

not travel fast, but they covered the miles to Wilton Abbey before nightfall.

The guard knocked on the abbey door. A nun opened the door and was terrified to find armed men on her doorstep. Seeing her horrified expression, Prince Henry jumped down from his horse to speak to her.

"Sister, please allow me to introduce myself. I am Prince Henry and as per the king's instructions, I have escorted these fine ladies to your abbey."

The nun, having had a moment to catch her breath, looked at Edith and Mary, who'd been helped down from their mounts.

"The princesses have arrived?"

"Indeed," Henry said. His beaming smile had the nun flushing pink.

"I shall notify the abbess. If you will please wait here, my lord."

Edith came to stand at Henry's side.

"You've gone from terrifying her to making her half in love with you," she commented.

He grinned down at her. "I did nothing," he said innocently. "What a shocking thing to say, Princess Edith."

"Not the most shocking gossip I've heard about you."

His eyebrow arched, daring her to go on.

Never one to back down from a challenge, Edith said, "I've heard you are a womanizer and more than one nun has cast aside their veil to be with you."

He threw his head back and laughed.

"You do not deny it," she said, casting an accusing glance his way.

"I am merely surprised that news of my exploits has reached even your innocent ears."

Her mouth pinched. She'd been hoping to catch him off guard and embarrass him. Quite the opposite. He was grinning from ear to ear.

"Let me assure you I have never sullied my reputation by seducing a nun. I am a God-fearing man."

"That is good to hear," Edith said primly, and earned herself another smile.

"You'd make a good abbess."

She wasn't sure if she should feel insulted or not. One never knew with him. Realizing they wouldn't have much time, she turned to ask, "Have you had any news from my uncle or brother?"

Henry's face grew serious. "No. But neither do I hear anything bad. They are gathering allies to their cause."

"Do you think Edgar will take the throne?"

"Your uncle is a wily man. He's a good general with a strong reputation. There's no better commander. He will ensure no harm comes to your brother."

"That doesn't answer my question."

He grinned. "I cannot predict the future, princess. I certainly hope he will and pray for his success."

The abbess arrived, flocked by the prioress and another high-ranking nun. Henry bowed to them and made introductions.

"You are most welcome, Prince Henry." She smiled kindly upon him before turning the same warm expression to Edith and Mary. "You've been expected. What an honor we have to be able to house you here."

"Thank you, Reverend Mother," Edith said, curtsying politely.

"Prioress Ursula shall show you to your rooms. You will want to rest and eat something after such a long journey." All business now, the abbess turned to the prince and extended him the invitation to eat something before pressing on.

"Unfortunately, this journey has already been delayed far too long. We shall return to Westminster at this very moment."

"I understand. You have such pressing matters to see to." The abbess nodded her head, then reached out to another nun, who handed her a sealed letter. "If you could deliver this to your brother, the king, I would be grateful to you."

"Of course, Reverend Mother." Henry nodded his head and tucked the letter into the purse that hung from his belt. "You may entrust this letter with me. Farewell." And without further delay, he returned to his horse. In one graceful movement he was back in the saddle.

Edith's eyes followed the retinue until they disappeared out of view.

Only the cart remained, and that would be going back to Westminster tomorrow.

The abbess of Wilton Abbey was a woman in her mid-forties named Hawise. She was allegedly the bastard daughter of King Harold II. No one was sure, but the rumors persisted because of the handsome endowment given to the abbey on her behalf. Years later, she was appointed abbess.

Edith was pleasantly surprised to find the table set with

all sorts of food that Cristina had forbidden them. Pastries and fish cooked in thick sauces filled the platters. There was no shortage of candied fruits and nuts either.

"As you are not nuns, you are entitled to eat meat and I can order some cooked for you if you like," the abbess said, inviting them to sit.

Fine linen covered the table and Edith felt she was underdressed for such a fine banquet. Clearly, the abbess had a taste for the finer things in life. Nor, did she appear to be as strict as Cristina had been.

"That will not be necessary, but thank you," Edith said. She didn't wish to cause the nunnery more trouble.

"I was told your aunt was very harsh with you. Rest assured the king would not thank me if you remained waifish while you stayed in my care. Nor if you grew too serious."

Edith and Mary glanced at each other.

"I assure you that neither of us has a gloomy or serious disposition. Our long travel here has sapped us of our good humor. Forgive us."

Hawise waved away her apologies. "There is nothing to forgive, my dear daughters. After you have eaten, Alise over there shall escort you to your rooms and ensure you have everything you could need. We shall pamper you as the princesses you are."

"Will we have horses we can ride?" Mary asked. She had noticed the extensive stables.

Hawise dabbed at the corner of her lips with a napkin. "When a suitable escort can be arranged. We also keep our mews well stocked. I am fond of hawking myself."

Edith's eyes widened at that.

"We might not have great relics to display to pilgrims, but we are a godly house and close to the king's lands. In fact, we are on the very border of one of his deer parks. The royal party often stays at the hunting lodge nearby. The king always honors us by coming to pray here whenever he can spare a moment from his duties."

"Ah," Edith said, looking down at her plate. The extravagance of this little banquet made sense now. This abbey was convenient for the king to keep a close eye on them, and it was on his usual route so he and his friends might stop in at any moment.

Edith and Mary ate their fill and then excused themselves.

Their chambers at Wilton were grander than at Romsey, but this did not please her as much as it should have. A tapestry depicting a prowling lion hung in their chamber, and Edith felt it was she who was being hunted. She had her own bedroom with a feather bed and pillow that were far more comfortable than what she had slept on since leaving Scotland.

A knock at her door interrupted her train of thought. A moment later, Mary popped her head in.

"What beautiful rooms we have," she said. "But I will miss sleeping beside you."

"Will you indeed?" Edith snorted. "I recall you complaining I kicked all night."

Mary grinned and glanced around Edith's chamber.

"Your tapestry is much finer than mine."

"You can have it. There's something terrifying about the beast."

ELEVEN

Life at Wilton quickly fell into routine. Prayer determined the flow of the day. They attended Lauds at dawn and then after a light meal prepared to hear Prime. When they weren't at prayer with the nuns, they were left largely to their own devices. They were considered guests rather than actual residents at the nunnery.

Edith was sure this meant the king intended their stay to be of short duration.

With that in mind she kept up the appearance of being an overly devout young woman with a heart meant for the church rather than the secular world.

She was scrupulous about attending Mass and maintained a serious composure at all times. It was a struggle, Wilton Abbey provided many temptations. If she wished Edith could enjoy hawking, dancing or watching the mummers that were hired to entertain important guests.

Indeed, Wilton operated as a way station for travelers. The guesthouse was built separate from the monastic cloister and church but still on the abbey's lands. The rooms were richly kept and meticulously maintained. Even the larder was stocked with fine wines and exotic spices to cater to the tastes of their often noble guests.

Given the number of visitors they received, merchants frequently came to sell their wares. An impromptu market was often set up right outside the heavy gates of the abbey. On May Day, musicians were hired and played while the local people danced and celebrated the coming spring.

Of course, it would've been improper for the nuns to attend such festivities, but Edith and her sister were encouraged to go.

Edith's stubborn refusal to partake in such pleasures frustrated Mary to no end.

"Edith, please. I long to see what the vendors have on display. The Reverend Mother said the king has provided her with a stipend for us and believes we should be more richly attired. Just think of something softer than this rough wool," Mary said, tugging at her mantle as if to make a point.

"If you think this is rough wool, then you have never been forced to wear a hairshirt to do penance. I didn't expect you to be so vain, Mary. A dress is nothing to freedom."

Mary frowned. "Do we have freedom? We cannot leave the abbey or receive visitors without permission. I have even less freedom than you because you refuse to allow me to the market and so I am confined by your whims as well as the king's."

"Which of us is truly free? Even the king must heed God's command. He cannot simply do as he chooses."

"You may be happy to die an old maid, but I am not." Mary sneered and left the room, slamming the door behind her.

With a heavy heart, Edith turned to her needlework. Every stitch was a prayer for patience.

A reprieve came from a most unexpected quarter. Edith and Mary were walking in the inner courtyard composing a poem when they heard a familiar voice call out to them.

Edith spun around and grinned when she spotted her brother. "Edgar!" She ran to him in a most unladylike fashion and then, remembering herself, came to an abrupt stop and curtsied properly to him before taking his hand in hers.

"What news? Are you well? I thought you were in Scotland?"

Edgar laughed. "Your questions are like a volley of arrows that blot out the sun."

"Have you really faced such a thing?" Mary asked. She'd caught up to them.

"If he has, I'm sure he will pay a bard handsomely to compose a ballad about it," Prince Henry said, approaching the siblings.

Edith's smile fell at the sight of him. She wondered why he was here yet again.

"My brother is a brave soldier. I am sure he would stoically face down such a threat."

"Then I would have to call him a fool," Henry said, with a shake of his head. "No soldier, no matter how well armored, could face such an onslaught and come out unscathed."

His eyes met hers, full of challenge. But Edith didn't rise to the provocation and simply swung back to her brother.

"I am so glad you have come."

"You may not be once you know I come bearing sad tidings. Our aunt Cristina has died. The king wrote to inform me," Edgar said.

"Oh," Edith said, surprised that this expected news still shocked her. "Though I am glad to know that she no longer suffers. I've prayed for her recovery every night since we left Romsey. Later, I shall ask the Reverend Mother if we could hold a special vigil for her soul."

"That is kind of you, sister," Edgar said, nodding his approval.

"Well, I am eager to hear the rest of your news," Edith hurried to say. "There is plenty of food and drink if you are hungry, or there is a pretty orchard we might walk through if you wish."

"Lead the way."

"Or the market," Mary jumped in to say.

Edith frowned at her, but Edgar liked that even more. "We rode past it on the way here. There was even an acrobat."

"Oh, please let's go," Mary whined.

Edith had no choice but to agree.

The four of them ventured out of Wilton Abbey's gate. Despite herself, Edith felt a growing sense of excitement.

There were so many people wandering about that it took a while to adjust. They took their time examining the stalls. Some sold religious trinkets, ribbons, and cloth, others hard cheeses and other delicacies.

Her brother, eyeing some of the braided pastries, couldn't resist buying a few. They decided to make a picnic of it. Under the shade of a large oak tree the four of them sat, enjoying the flaky layers stuffed with candied walnuts, raisins, and suet.

"It's delicious," Edgar said. "It beats the food we can get while on campaign."

"Has our uncle returned from Scotland too?" Edith asked, nibbling at the crust of her pie.

"No, he stayed behind, shoring up support and determining our strategy. It will be a close battle, but there's no avoiding it now. Duncan's wife gave birth to a stillborn girl. It would be best to act soon before he has a nursery full of contenders to the throne." Edgar spoke with the coldness of a soldier. Edith couldn't help recoiling, even though she knew this was the way of the world. She had no love in her heart for Ethelreda, but she was sorry for the loss she had suffered.

"For now we haven't done much but raided and engaged in a few minor skirmishes. But I'm making a name for myself, and as my reputation grows, more nobles will flock to my side. Our father shall be avenged."

"Duncan did not kill him," Edith said, her voice a soft whisper that Edgar did not hear. But Prince Henry did. His gaze fell upon her again.

"Perhaps that is not the right choice of words, Prince Edgar. However, your cause is just and should you succeed I am certain you shall usher in an era of peace and prosperity for Scotland."

Edgar shifted. "Yes. You are right."

"Will you stay for the summer festival? The Reverend Mother promised she would hire musicians and a troupe of actors to play for us," Mary interjected. This small taste of freedom had made her long for more.

"I can only stay the night. We are on our way to meet with the king. Prince Henry's brother has promised us further funds and men to join my cause."

"What does he want in exchange for this?" Edith asked.

Edgar frowned at his sister. Perhaps the women he was used to didn't question him like this.

Henry laughed. "Your sister has the astute mind of a politician."

Edgar's cheeks turned pink. Edith noted how he had changed and cropped his hair short in the Norman style. Was he simply hoping to ingratiate himself with his Norman allies or had he become a supplicant to them?

"It is merely what is my due. Duncan stole the throne from us. Edmund has proven himself to be a traitor and Duncan is an illegitimate bastard. King William Rufus knows God favors my just claim."

"The Pope's cause is just." Edith ripped a piece of the pie and popped it into her mouth. The sugar melting on her tongue. "Will he really give you the money and men when he has sworn to provide whatever he can to the Crusade? I merely ask because I am ignorant of the ways of the world." She spoke sweetly, but she could sense her brother's growing discomfort.

"The king will do right by your family," Prince Henry said. "It suits his purpose and shores up his own borders. It's far better to have friends at your back than raiders.

147

Northumberland has sent envoys to the court of your half-brother. We believe the pair of them have made an alliance to attack England."

"But his rebellion was put down," Edith said, frowning.

"Yes, and he swore fealty to King William Rufus. However, he is a false man and will rise again. He might succeed if he has the Scottish army to help him. Therefore, my brother would rather have a new king in Scotland who is less sympathetic to Northumberland."

Edgar nodded. "Exactly."

"I am glad to hear it." There was an edge of falseness to her words. The way Henry had laid everything out made Edgar once again beholden to King William Rufus. Would Scotland simply become an extension of England?

"I long for the day I can return to Scotland." She said this casually, but watched her brother carefully.

His expression was unreadable as he reached over and patted her hand. "I know, sister. As do I, I assure you."

They returned to browsing the market stalls. Before they turned back to the abbey, their brother purchased matching ribbons to braid into their hair. Edith had chosen ones dyed a pale yellow while her sister had gone for a bright crimson silk.

"You chose wisely," Prince Henry said. "They will look striking against your black hair."

Edith flushed, knowing she'd been thinking of her appearance when choosing the ribbon rather than focusing on practicality. Her sister had teased her for making such a plain choice, but Edith had known that the yellow would suit her best. Her sister was more concerned with the beauty of the red ribbon and hadn't yet realized the crimson would get lost among the reddish gold tinge of her tresses.

"I didn't even want the ribbons, but Edgar insisted."

"You are scrupulous in your determination to avoid enjoyment," Henry commented lightly.

Edith scowled. "If I am, then you are just as determined to watch life pass you by."

He raised an eyebrow in surprise. Before he could ask her what she meant, she turned her back to him, not wishing to risk insulting a Prince of England further. Putting some distance between them, she pretended a woven scarf had caught her attention.

They returned to the abbey and the abbess informed them they would dine in private that evening. Edgar and Henry went out hawking and returned with a fine catch of quail and a rabbit for their dinner.

The following day, Mary and Edith bid their brother farewell.

"I shall pray day and night for your success," Edith said, curtsying to him before embracing him. She meant it too. At the very least, if Edgar won the throne of Scotland, she and Mary would be free to return to their true home. Once there she was sure that Edgar wouldn't force her to marry someone she didn't like.

Mary stepped forward, tears brimming in the corners of her eyes as she said her goodbyes.

Out of courtesy, Edith bid Henry farewell, too.

"Thank you, Princess Edith. I hope I shall find a way to stop offending you in the future." He grinned at her stunned expression and moved on quickly before she could make any retort.

Edith gritted her teeth, reminding herself that she was a princess of Scotland and had to maintain her composure at all times. She wouldn't be baited like a bear.

As they rode off, Edith waved, her eyes fixed on her brother's retreating form. Mary wiped the corners of her eyes.

"Come now, Mary, you know better than to cry like this," Edith said, but wrapped an arm around her sister's shoulders.

Mary sniffed. "I had a taste of the finer things in life and now I don't know if I can go back to the dull life of the cloister."

Taken aback, Edith was compelled to promise her that she would be less strict in the future. "If the Reverend Mother allows it, we shall go out into the village more, I promise."

PART THREE
1097

TWELVE

The campaign in Scotland was progressing well. Every day news of some small victory reached Edith's ears. She could practically taste the freedom.

Unfortunately, these victories drew the King of England's interest in Edith once again. As the chance of their brother ascending to the throne rose, so did her perceived value as a bride.

Edith's worst fears were realized when the Earl of Surrey appeared at the abbey. Lord William Warren was a tall, handsome man. He was high in the king's favor and boasted an impressive lineage. His mother was the daughter of William the Conqueror and, as a cousin to the king, had close familial ties. More importantly, he had a solid claim to the throne.

Everyone suspected the king intended to name the earl as his heir, even though he had two living brothers. If it came to a fight, the earl had far more resources than either

Henry did or his bankrupt brother, Robert, Duke of Normandy.

In many ways Lord William was a catch. But Edith was immediately put off.

He saw her as yet another way to bolster his reputation and strengthen his claim to the throne. He must have been aware that through her mother, she had royal English blood in her veins, and if Edgar won his throne he would receive a substantial dowry and yet another ally.

He had no interest in her beyond what she could provide him. He made that clear the moment he greeted her with the way his attention immediately went past her, as if winning her approval had never crossed his mind. Indeed, what she wanted or liked did not matter. If the king commanded her to wed him, she would have no choice but to obey.

It was humiliating and grated on her sense of pride.

The abbess was flattered to receive the earl and promised to order a great banquet in his honor at the guesthouse.

"Of course, I look forward to a good meal." William smiled benignly. He glanced around and happened upon Edith standing at a polite distance with her sister, Mary. "And the Princess Edith will be joining us as well, won't she? I have heard such wonderful stories of her skills as a hostess."

Edith stiffened. Was he mocking her?

Before she could think of some excuse to avoid going to the feast, the abbess answered on her behalf. "She would be grateful for the opportunity to dine with men of such high rank. It's a compliment you should even think of her. Myself and the prior will be there as well."

"Excellent," Lord William said, his lips curling into a pleasant smile. "Now, I hear that the deer parks near here are wonderful."

"Yes, my lord." The abbess hesitated.

"Fear not, the king allows me to hunt where I please. I shall pay him for every stag I kill."

Edith frowned at his hubris while the abbess simpered and smiled. "As you please, my lord."

He left with his retinue of men in tow, only casting one more glance Edith's way. There was a hint of displeasure on his features as he regarded her.

While Abbess Hawise wouldn't tolerate the antics of her wearing a nun's habit, Edith had taken to wearing a plain coif. The white linen material hid her hair and made her features appear severe. She supposed she wasn't the beautiful princess he had envisioned.

The moment he was out of earshot Hawise rounded on her.

"Go get dressed in something nicer and let down your hair. Think of the honor you have in being singled out by such a great man."

Edith remained rigidly noncompliant. "I am not some serving wench."

Hawise let out a puff of air, frustrated by her stubbornness and not for the first time. She wagged a finger in her face. "Listen to me, Princess Edith. You shall dine with his lordship. It was his express wish that you do so. You clearly don't have your best interest at heart. The man is unmarried and he has clearly set his sights on you. The king would not have allowed him to come here if he didn't support the match."

Edith was ready to argue when she caught sight of another arrival at the abbey. It was Prince Henry, looking weary, on a borrowed mount. His cloak was fraying at the edges and stained with splatters of mud. The abbess pursed her lips for a moment, thinking he was some beggar. However, upon recognizing him, she moved forward to greet him. Edith took the chance to escape.

Once in her rooms, she stomped around, fuming that she was expected to make herself appealing to Lord William. It was an insult to her dignity.

Mary followed in after her and sat on the edge of her bed, watching her with amusement. "I don't understand why you are so upset. He's such a handsome man, and did you see how he jumped from his horse?" Her sister sighed dreamily. "The abbess is right. He honors you."

Edith was far from honored, but she clamped her lips tightly together. Mary didn't understand her. When it came to the subject of marriage, they had vastly different opinions.

"If he asked me to marry him, I would accept him right away," Mary said as she combed Edith's hair.

"He has not asked me," Edith pointed out.

"If you don't make a mess of things, I'm sure he will. Even the abbess believes he has only come here because he intends to ask the king for your hand in marriage."

Edith rolled her eyes. "Edgar will have his throne soon enough and we shall be back under his guardianship. William Warren will have to ask him for permission, and I will be sure Edgar doesn't grant it."

Silence stretched between them as Mary regarded her with genuine surprise. She set down the comb. "Edith. The king will not allow us to go whether or not Edgar is successful."

Edith opened her mouth to protest, but the truth of it hit her. She'd been a fool. A damned fool. The moment they had crossed the border five years ago, they had placed themselves at the mercy of the English King. He was an opportunistic man and would not relinquish the wardship of two princesses. Even David, their youngest brother, was in his household and a hostage for Edgar's continued good behavior. If their brother failed to take the crown, they'd all still be useful pawns.

Edith clenched her hands into fists. She wouldn't go meekly. Not when it was not her choice. She wanted the freedom to determine her own future. No one else.

Mary left to tend to her own toilette. Her sister took far more pride in her appearance than Edith ever did. When she emerged from her chamber, she was dressed in a fashionable russet gown, with a gilded girdle around her waist. She'd braided her hair into two long braids with the red ribbon Edgar had purchased for her.

Between the two of them she was the one who looked like a potential bride. But she was younger, and thus she would have to wait until after Edith was married. For a moment Edith pitied her sister.

"You still manage to look like a nun." Mary frowned at her.

"The abbess cannot complain. I'm wearing my best gown. And don't even bother trying to offer me one of yours. They are far too small and long for me," Edith said triumphantly.

The dress she wore was a size too big. It hung about her frame loosely, hiding her figure from view. She had replaced her plain linen wimple for one made of silky gauze, but the effect was still the same.

Where her sister had chosen bracelets and a chain to adorn herself, Edith wore only a large cross on a gold chain. The very picture of a devout princess.

They sat working on some embroidery until a servant came to escort them to the guesthouse.

Even from far away, they could hear the sounds of merriment inside.

A wave of anxiety and shyness threatened to overcome Edith, and she hesitated in the corridor to the hall.

"It won't deter him overly much," a familiar voice called out to her.

She steeled herself to face Prince Henry. "My Lord Henry, what a pleasure to see you again. I didn't think you'd be here." Her tone was syrupy and false. From the smirk on his face, he knew it too.

"And miss the opportunity for a meal? You don't know me at all."

Edith frowned at him. He should be ashamed of himself, but he'd long ago accepted the fact he was an impoverished prince with very little prospects. In fact, he wore it like a badge of honor. Not that it stopped him from enjoying the privilege of his position. He competed in tournaments, rode to war, and, if rumors she'd heard were true, had several mistresses.

"I don't know you at all," she said haughtily.

He smiled at that and with a wave of his hand invited her to enter the hall first. Never a coward, Edith strode in with Mary following at her heels.

The abbess motioned her over and Lord William bowed to her, placing a courtly kiss on the back of her hand. Edith fought the urge to wipe her hand on her dress.

He invited her to take the seat on his right in one of the high-back chairs. The air was fragrant with the scent of stewed meat and freshly baked bread.

A bard sang a wonderful ballad about Saint George slaying the dragon while servants expertly weaved in and out between the tables laid out for the visitors. They deposited platters of food and jugs of wine on the tables before disappearing to fetch more from the kitchens.

Edith watched all this with a sense of longing. It was far more stimulating than the dull monotony of the refectory. Many nuns ate in silence and the food was often uninspiring and cold. Depriving the body was meant to help enlighten the soul.

Someone recalled how a knight had fallen off his horse in a tournament and everyone laughed at the embarrassed man. The general lively energy and excitement in the hall reminded Edith of her parents court.

Her mother had been a great queen, who shared in her husband's power. She heard petitions from tenant farms and minor lords, and she oversaw the finances of the household. There were also the ceremonial roles she was expected to play, as well as hunting, hawking, and dancing.

It reminded Edith how different life outside a nunnery could be. She half-closed her eyes, listening to the uplifting ballad, only to spy musicians waiting in the wings. There would be dancing later and the thought didn't strike her with terror as it usually did.

She might be willing to trade the peace of the nunnery for this, but would she be willing to shackle herself to this man? From beneath her lashes she studied William Warren more closely.

He was well built, with even unmarred features. She had no trouble believing he was a powerful magnate. But he was cold. And just like that, caution overcame her enthusiasm for the evening. There was a cruelness and indifference in his eyes that she did not like.

She imagined he would be a demanding husband and then quick to abandon her once he had taken everything he wanted from her. He was not the sort of man who would honor and respect her. He merely wanted her for the prestige it would give him and for the sons she might bear him.

"How was the hunt, my lord?" she asked him demurely.

He sniffed. "We caught a deer. The cooks have been preparing it all afternoon for our meal. I have promised you shall have the best cut as a sign of my esteem."

Edith's smile was tight. "How generous. I am surprised you didn't bring down a stag." Her tone was neutral so he couldn't accuse her of insulting him, but even so he frowned.

"I suppose the fault must be placed with your hounds for not sniffing out a better quarry." She played with the cross hanging from her neck as she watched him.

She could see the moment the barb found its mark. He stilled and studied her, seeing past her royal lineage, and the unflattering gown, to the person behind it. She was a force to be reckoned with he could see that now.

Her lip curled in a triumphant smile. "In any case, I must warn your lordship that I abhor decadence. I prefer to eat simply. Fish and the like to food such as this," she said with a wave of her hand to the plates of food in front of them.

"Surely, my lady, you jest," Lord William said, reaching for a goblet of wine. He looked past her to the abbess sitting beside her with a pinched expression, having heard the whole conversation.

Edith turned to look at Hawise. "I have been raised in a nunnery for the majority of my life. One might say I have grown accustomed to the life in one. I fear I must confess I am jealous of the position God has called you to." She turned her face upward, clasping her hands in front of her as if sending a prayer to almighty God. Then she scratched her neck. Revealing the pièce de résistance of her outfit for the briefest moment. Beneath her fine dress, she'd worn a hairshirt.

William Warren, who'd been watching her so closely, gritted his teeth at the sight of it.

The abbess too said a prayer under her breath.

"I find it hard to believe that a young pious woman such as yourself would—would mortify your flesh. What sins could you have committed to earn such a harsh penance?" he asked, his tone full of horror.

Edith faced him. "No amount of penance will wash away my sins. For are all women and men not born in sin? Had I been born a man I might have taken up the cross and gone on Crusade. Since I was not, I am left with this."

Abbess Hawise, having finally gotten over her shock, said, "You must pardon her, my lord. As she has said, she has been very strictly raised. Her aunt was famous for her rigid adherence to her faith. I'm afraid she ingrained that same fanaticism into her niece. But rest assured she only needs a gentle hand to show her there are other ways one can accomplish God's will."

William Warren gulped down the rest of his wine.

"I find it hard to believe a young woman would feel the resort to such extreme measures of piety."

Edith bowed her head penitently. "I am the king's loyal subject." Politically, she didn't specify which king. She hoped that God would forgive her the omission. "But I also suffer from excessive pride. It makes my heart bleed to think that no matter what I do, I will never achieve the perfection of Mary, mother of God."

"You speak of your piety as though it were some flaw you possess. It's almost as though you believe such a quality would make you a less desirable wife," he said.

She merely laughed, undulating her voice so the sound was high-pitched. She was pleased to see him fight back a wince. "My lord, quite the opposite. I long for a husband who would encourage me to look after my immortal soul." She batted her lashes in his direction for good measure.

If it weren't for everything else, this might have been seen as a coquettish gesture rather than yet another challenge. The gauntlet was thrown and William Warren was uninterested.

"Silence is another virtue," he said under his breath, reaching for the wine again.

She laughed, covering her mouth with the wide sleeve of her gown. "Then I shall make sure to practice it."

For the remainder of the meal she sat back in her seat,

picking at the food on her plate even as she yearned to eat more. Lord William quickly lost interest in her and was talking of the hunting with his friend on his left.

It was only when Prince Henry entered the chamber that Lord William immediately perked up. Edith noted that he did not stand, even though Henry was theoretically his superior by rank. It was an insult to Henry but one William could afford to make.

"Prince Henry, I did not know you were staying at Wilton."

All conversation stopped and everyone's attention flew to the prince and the earl. The tension in the room was palpable as Henry stepped forward, having not uttered a word.

Edith had never seen him outside the company of her brother and uncle. They had always treated him with respect. This was the first time she saw proof of his status as "*the beggar prince.*" Pity swelled in her chest for him, but she had to give him credit. He did not back down. If anything, there was something intimidating about the way he stared down Lord William. He appeared unconcerned.

"Wilton Abbey is famous for its hospitality," he said. "I am often tempted to stop by here as I travel around the country."

Lord William's lips twisted in a mocking smile. "How lucky for you that you are able to go about your business untethered by pressing responsibilities. It's only a pity you do not have your own great houses to stay at when you— travel about," William said, with a chuckle.

Edith's eyes went wide at the way he threw such terrible insults at Henry. How could he bear it? What she hated most of all was the way William was deriving so much pleasure from embarrassing him.

But rather than backing down without a fight, Henry merely shrugged. "We cannot all have had your luck—" He stopped mid-sentence, tilting his head. "Remind me how your older brother died? There was talk of assassination but it might have been raiders in Ireland."

William flushed but recovered himself. "Come now, cousin, let us not talk about such terrible things in the presence of such delicate ladies. Enjoy the feast. Tomorrow, if you wish, you may join my company when we go hunting. I am sure we have a horse to spare for you."

"I will take you up on your offer. I'm a better hunter than you. The deer you caught was thin and sickly, hardly worth gracing this fine table," Henry said.

For a brief moment Henry caught Edith's eye, and she looked down to hide her amusement.

At her side, she felt William tense, but rather than respond he made a flourish of his arm and a servant came forward with a chair. He pointed to one of the emptier tables, far from the high table. Yet another insult that Henry bore with surprising patience and confidence. As he took his seat and began piling food on his plate, when he looked up and caught her watching him again. Edith was quick to turn her gaze back to the entertainment.

The bard finished his performance and, setting aside his lute, picked up his lyre. He sang a French song of warm summer days. The tension dissipated and everyone began to enjoy themselves again.

Once the bard finished, Lord William Warren threw him a coin. His eyes, however, were fixed on Henry to make sure he saw. *See how generous I can afford to be. You are nothing to me.*

Edith caught the determined look in Henry's eye as he got to his feet. William's hand flew to his belt as though he were itching to grab his sword.

Henry didn't approach the high table but rather the bard.

The bard handed him the lute and Henry strung the instrument. He turned to address the abbess. "Since I have nothing with which to repay your kind hospitality, I shall entertain you instead."

Edith was surprised by the powerful timbre of his voice. He played elegantly and when he was finished the guests applauded him.

William Warren's lips pursed in displeasure. Then, smirking, he said, "Well done, my lord. I find I must reward you as well." He reached into his coin purse and threw a coin towards the prince.

Henry caught it midair and smiled, though there was a dangerous edge to it.

He handed the lute back to the bard and then loudly, for all to hear, said, "Thank you, for lending me your fine instrument," before placing the coin into the bard's hands. With one last sweeping bow to the crowd, he returned to his seat.

William's nostrils flared, his hands gripping his fork tightly.

Edith felt that only the bard benefited from this exchange. William and Henry were like bulls squaring off for a battle neither could win.

At the abbess' direction a troupe of minstrels took the

place of the bard. They began to play a lively song, while the tables in the center of the room were cleared away to make room for dancing.

William Warren glanced Edith's way once, as if considering if he wished to ask her to dance but couldn't find it within himself to do it. The abbess was having none of it, however.

"Princess Edith, might you not dance with your sister? It would please the company to see you enjoying yourself."

"Reverend Mother, I would prefer not to—"

"I will have to add my weight behind her entreaty," Lord William interrupted, with a satisfied grin. He meant to catch her off guard and perhaps embarrass her. After all, what convent-raised woman would be a good dancer?

Edith itched to show him just how graceful and light-footed she could be. However, she had to force down her pride. One moment of triumph would undermine her plan of scaring him off.

"Then how could I refuse?" She stood and Mary shot out of her seat.

Yet Mary regarded her with displeasure as they moved around the table to the dance floor.

"You're making a spectacle of yourself and disgracing the both of us," she hissed under her breath as they began the steps.

Edith rolled her eyes. As they moved through the steps, Edith found she didn't have to work hard to make herself fumble and trip. The hairshirt scratched at her as they danced and she longed for the chance to remove it.

She noted dryly that the earl had lost interest in watching her quickly. *Oh to be a man*, she thought bitterly.

But all was going quite according to plan. As the dance continued, she caught sight of Prince Henry sitting at one of the lower tables. He was laughing at something his companion was saying, but his eyes caught hers for a moment and he tipped his head to her.

In acknowledgement?

She bit her lower lip and missed another step. Her sister would've run into her had she not moved fast to catch her.

Would Henry speak to Lord William after? Would he tell him that this was all a bit of playacting on her part? Why had he come? Why couldn't he have been delayed by even a day?

"Edith." Her sister pinched her wrist. With her attention back on her steps, her anxious thoughts ceased. When the music ended, they came to a stop and curtsied to the abbess and Lord William.

They were not asked for a repeat performance and the two sisters returned to their seats. Lord William graced her with a smile. "You aren't quite the uncouth peasant you claim you are. I wager you dance better than most nuns."

That stung, but she deserved it.

"I appreciate you saying so. It's true that of all pastimes dancing is one I enjoy and hope to do more of in the future."

His smile looked strained, but he didn't comment or mention marriage again.

Edith was able to excuse herself not long after, claiming she felt the need to pray.

Abbess Hawise was at her wits' end but let her go. How could she refuse? Edith had done her duty.

The following day Edith made sure to be in the chapel before dawn and piously prayed all day. She wore the hairshirt again and an angry red welt was now visible on her neck.

Lord William had greeted her during Mass and watched her from afar, but he appeared to have lost all interest in her as a bride. She hoped he would return to the king's court and forget all about her.

THIRTEEN

Edith was working in the alehouse, preparing another batch of malt with Sister Greta, when Mary stormed in, her expression a mixture of both excitement and anger.

"Mary? What is it?" Edith set down the wood spoon and approached.

"Abbess Hawise commands you to come to her in her rooms. She has news to give you."

"Very well," Edith said. With a hesitant shrug, she removed her apron and washed her hands. "Sister Greta, I will return as soon as I am able."

"Nonsense, Princess Edith, be on your way. Grace and I can handle things here."

Once outside the brewhouse, Edith looked at Mary. "You clearly know what this news is. Are you going to keep me in the dark?"

Mary's lips thinned. "You brought this upon yourself. You always think of yourself and not of how it might affect others."

"Whatever do you mean?" Fear shot through Edith. Had Lord William asked for Mary's hand instead? He was the king's favorite. Perhaps he'd made an exception.

Mary was close to tears and could not bring herself to speak or perhaps refused to.

They arrived at the Charterhouse to find Abbess Hawise sitting in judgment upon a tenant farmer who had failed to pay rents for a second time.

"We cannot allow this, John. You were given a reprieve last quarter. Now you have a fresh tale of sorrow to spring upon my ears," the abbess said, with a mournful shake of her head. "I hope you shall repent of your sins in confession. But I am afraid I cannot offer you another extension. You and your family will have to vacate your farm by the end of tomorrow."

"Reverend Mother, please have mercy," the farmer said, falling to his knees.

"Mercy?" Hawise's eyes flashed with anger. "Pray to God to cleanse your soul. Do you think news of your gambling has not reached my ears? Could that be the true reason for your failure to pay your rents? Regardless, I have made my decision. I hope you will learn from this."

The man, red-faced, knew he had no recourse. He stood and left.

The abbess whispered something to her clerk and then glanced at Edith.

"Ah, there you are. Come forward," she said, motioning with her hand. "I have received a letter from the king. Or rather the king's court." She placed a hand on the letter in front of her. Edith caught sight of the seal and wondered at the need for such formality.

"The king is greatly distressed to hear that the meeting with Lord William Warren didn't go as planned. Lord William is intent on contracting a marriage with a more amenable woman." The abbess paused as if she was waiting for Edith to be stricken by grief at the news. She pursed her lips together when she saw no outpouring of regret would be forthcoming. "He worries over the state of your well-being and has written to me to ensure that in the future you will behave as a lady of your station ought to. The king has also written to the archbishop on your behalf and they both instruct you to put away your hairshirt. In the meantime, he has made arrangements for your sister Mary to be removed from your company."

Edith's eyes went wide. She turned to glance at Mary, who was standing rigidly at her side.

"Ah, that's caught your attention, has it?" Hawise let out an exasperated sigh. "His Grace is sending Lady Mary to the House of Lady Phillipa De Lacy. She will take over guardianship of your sister and ensure you do not influence her with your behavior."

Edith choked on her own protest. Her hand reached for her sister's, as it always did in times of danger, but found herself to be repudiated. Coldness spread through her veins. There was nothing she could do to stop this. Nothing. The overwhelming sense of powerlessness made her feel faint.

"Your brother will be informed of these events as well. The king trusts that he will agree with his decision," the abbess said, as if guessing that Edith hoped the opposite.

"I do not wish to be separated from my sister," Edith pleaded.

"It is done," Abbess Hawise said. "Perhaps it is for the

best. I shall provide her with a chaperone and the king is
sending a retinue of his trusted men to escort her to her new
home."

"When?" Edith asked, her mouth dry.

"That I do not know. Perhaps in a few days or weeks,"
the abbess said with a shrug. "Be grateful you have time to
say your farewells." Then she dismissed them with a wave
of her hand.

Outside, Edith grabbed Mary by the shoulders, forcing
her sister to look her in the eye. "Mary, I am so sorry. I had
not thought he would punish you for my transgressions."

Mary glared. "That is your problem. You never think of
others, only yourself." She looked away, avoiding Edith's
gaze. "Part of me is thrilled. I don't want to leave you, but I
long for a different life. You are happy here within the
abbey, but I—I wish for more. I want to have the chance to
dance and play music all day. I want to be courted and
praised for my beauty. Lady Phillipa will give me all those
things. I won't be closeted away from the world."

Edith felt her breath catch in her throat. Was this truly
what her sister wanted? Did she not see the dangers of such
a world?

"But—if we just wait. We will—"

Mary looked at her incredulously. "What tales have you
spun for yourself? We should be grateful we are here and
that the king continues to pay for our expenses."

Scoffing, Edith released her hold on her sister. "We are
pawns in his game of politics."

"As we would be anywhere else. Despite all your
learning you aren't quite the realist you pretend to be,"

Mary said. "Perhaps it's because you are the eldest sister. I have always been in the shadows. The afterthought."

"Don't you dare say that. Mother and father loved you. I love you."

Mary managed a small smile. "But they are gone and your opinion counts for little to the world at large. Until you have power and influence in your own right." She reached out, touching Edith's cheek, and wiped away the tears that Edith hadn't even realized she was shedding. "I treasure our bond. But it will not feed us or put clothes on our back. And I am tired of living a life in this state of uncertainty. If someone wished to marry me, I would leap at the chance."

"Even if they are very old?" Edith cracked a smile.

A soft laugh escaped Mary. "Well, perhaps not then. Even I have my standards."

They embraced.

"I shall miss you terribly. Promise you will write to me whenever you can."

"I promise," Mary said easily. "I shall make you jealous with all my stories about the latest fashions, the card games I play, and the songs I learn."

Mary left Wilton riding a beautiful silver-gray mare who was sure-footed and handsome. She took only essentials with her for the short ten-mile journey. The countess had written that she would be providing Mary with an appropriate wardrobe and she'd have little need for the plain dresses she'd worn at the nunnery. Edith was left to pick over Mary's old things. Some gowns she'd pull apart and resew to suit herself. Others would be donated to the poor.

Autumn descended upon Wilton. The landscape quickly became barren as the trees lost their leaves and the wheat was harvested from the fields. The dreariness outside magnified the loneliness Edith felt at the loss of her sister. She was never without company of the nuns, but it wasn't the same.

Strangely enough her solitude was broken by the arrival of Prince Henry at the abbey. He was on his way south from the north of England and had come carrying a message from her brother and uncle in Scotland.

It would be unseemly for them to meet alone, so Sister Katherine sat with them as Edith made a big show of working on embroidery while Henry relaxed by the fire drinking a cup of spice ale.

"I actually have two letters for you," he said. "Both your uncle and brother were in good health the last I saw them, so you needn't fear on that account."

"Good," Edith said, nipping at the thread and carelessly discarding the remaining scrap. She reached for the blue thread and began to work on the blue feathers of a bird when she felt his gaze on her.

"Aren't you going to ask for the letters?" he teased.

"You will give them to me in time," she replied. "I have learned a degree of patience since the last time you saw me."

"Ah yes, the buffoon attempted to court you. That was a sight to behold," Henry whispered.

Edith glanced toward Sister Katherine to find she had fallen asleep in her seat.

"He wasn't a buffoon," she hissed, leaning toward him.

Henry's brow arched. "Oh, so you were eager for his attention? My mistake." He craned his head to look out the oriel window at the darkening sky.

"You know very well I didn't care for his suit."

"Really?" Henry's eyes were full of mischievous energy.

Edith knew better than to rise to the bait, but at the same time she didn't see the harm in sharing her thoughts with him.

"We wouldn't have suited. He was far too proud."

He looked amused. "And you are not?"

She glared at him, which only made his smile deepen.

"Tell me I'm wrong, Princess Edith."

She was taken aback. "There's no sense answering you. No matter what I say, I will sound like a fool."

Sister Katherine stirred. Edith looked pointedly at him.

"Well, you should be on your way," Edith said, glancing out the window too. "A storm is bound to hit soon. Surely there's no reason for you to stay now that you've done your duty and visited me."

Silence stretched between them as his dark eyes scanned her face. "I told the king there was no use separating you from your sister."

"You did?" Edith asked genuinely surprised.

Henry nodded. "I knew it would make no difference to your resolve to reject all your suitors." That ghost of a smile was back on his lips. "Nor would it reform your character. Which I am happy to see is still intact." She frowned, but he went on. "All jests aside, I know how much you cared for each other and I am sorry she's been sent away."

"Even if I had played along and married the earl the

outcome would've been the same. I doubt she would've been able to live with me. So you see I considered my options quite carefully. Though I'll admit I hadn't expected the king to send her away. Mary writes to me she has been allowed to keep the mare and is enjoying her time among the noble ladies of her household. She's happy. Maybe things worked out for the best."

He considered her and nodded. "Except you are still here. Left alone, with no prospect of escape in sight."

Edith glanced at Sister Katherine, whose eyes were still shut.

Henry spoke again. "Let's put aside this pretension you will ever become a nun."

She whipped her head around. Ready to argue, but he put a hand to his lips to hush her. That sly smile returned.

"You are a strategist. If you had truly intended to take the veil, you would've found a way to do it by now." He cocked his head to the side. "One cannot help but admire how you weaseled your way out of two marriages. It also leaves me wondering what you are waiting for." He stroked the stubble growing across his jawline. She realized despite his good humor he was looking more haggard than usual.

"I don't believe that this conversation is entirely proper," she said, feeling flustered.

He leaned back in his seat, his attention fixed anywhere but on her and she returned to her needlework. After a time he reached into the satchel at his feet and pulled out two sealed letters. They were crumpled but unopened.

She took them from his outstretched hands, their fingertips touching for the briefest moment.

"Thank you. For what it's worth, I am sorry for how

Lord William treated you. You didn't deserve that. You are a prince of the realm regardless of whether or not you are landless."

"I'd forgotten about that." There was an edge of bitterness in his voice but he managed to shrug off his ill humor. "Lord William and I have been rivals since we were children. We never miss a chance to insult each other. If I were in his position I might had done the same." She nearly argued with him but stopped herself. "But there will come a time when we will have to set aside our differences and work together."

"What do you mean?" Edith asked, intrigued.

Henry merely shrugged. "There's always a war to be fought, rebels to be thwarted. When we march out together, we will be allies and will have to work together. He might be a vain jealous man, but he isn't a fool."

"But you just called him one not too long ago."

Sister Katherine let out a light snore, startled, and then sat up, eyes open.

"In some respects he is. However, I trust him to have my back on the battlefield and at the end of the day, that's all that matters." Henry got to his feet. He bowed to Edith and then turned to Sister Katherine. "I am afraid I have overstayed my welcome. Please forgive me, Sister. Now I will say my farewells and be off before night sets in."

"Y-yes, my lord," Sister Katherine stammered, trying to get her bearings. He bowed once more and then left the small solar.

If Sister Katherine noticed Edith barely progressed in her needlework, she didn't comment. With a yawn, she struggled to her feet, muttering under her breath about the comings and goings of young men.

Once she was gone, Edith set aside her embroidery and read her letters.

Both were of a similar nature. Her brother and uncle were happy to report that they'd made advancements with their campaign in Scotland. The King of England had kept his promise to send them funds and reinforcements. Now they were readying for one final push. There was no mention of Edmund and what Edgar would do with their eldest surviving traitor of a brother. Edith said a prayer that all would work itself out in the end. There was a small post-script on her uncle's letter urging her to be more careful about who she offended and that she should open her heart to the possibility that her life would change.

Edith wanted to toss the letter aside. She would wait. As they said in their letters, it was only a matter of time now before her brother sat on the throne. Things might be different in a few months.

———

Edith was summoned to Abbess Hawise's private rooms. By now weeks had passed since Henry's visit. A good harvest had been brought in and, as was custom, a banquet was held for all the abbey tenants and workers.

Edith entered the room and took a moment to admire the beautiful new tapestry hanging on the walls. It depicted the Annunciation to the Blessed Virgin Mary, when the Angel Gabriel visited and informed her she was going to give birth to the son of God. The colors were vibrant and dazzled her.

A gracious lord had gifted the expensive tapestry to the abbey. Not only had the abbey cared for her during her illness but the abbess had ordered the nuns to say special prayers over the barren woman before instructing her to go on pilgrimage to the Shrine of Our Lady at Walsingham. A year later, the gift had arrived with news that she had safely delivered a healthy baby boy. Given the couple, now in their mid-thirties, had lost hope of ever having a child, it was a miracle indeed.

Edith looked away from the tapestry to the Abbess Hawise, warming her hands by the fire. Her expression was unreadable as she said, "Princess Edith, please have a seat."

She obeyed, knowing that something monumental must have happened to warrant such a serious formal discussion.

"I am pleased to tell you the news I received from King William Rufus himself." She paused and Edith, who was already on the edge of her seat, felt her heart pound wildly in her chest. "There has been a great battle. By the grace of God, your brother and uncle have defeated your half-brother. The last we heard was they were riding to Edinburgh to take control of the capital. By now, it is believed your brother has been crowned."

Edith, incredulous at the news, crossed herself. "Thank God our prayers have been answered. Am I to return to Scotland?"

The abbess smiled kindly but shook her head. "I am afraid not, Princess Edith. You are to remain in our safe-keeping. Isn't this the life you prefer? You've praised the monastic life so often—"

Edith clenched her jaw. "Of course, Reverend Mother." She'd been expecting this, but it didn't ease the sting of it any more.

"I shall keep you abreast of any fresh developments."

"Is there any news about my brother Edmund? And Duncan? Were they taken prisoner?"

The abbess looked at her as though she should know better than to ask. "They died in the battle."

"Ah," Edith said, feeling queasy. It was one thing to know what might happen but quite another to have it confirmed. One brother could be just as ruthless as the other. It made her sick to think about. Then, steeling herself, she stood.

"Thank you for informing me, Reverend Mother." She curtsied. "I believe I must go pray now. I hope in death they find peace and that my brother Edgar's coming to the throne will usher in an era of peace and prosperity for Scotland, as well as continued friendship with England." Her speech was courtly, as befitting a royal princess. Edith hoped her words might curry favor with the King of England.

PART FOUR
1099

Fourteen

"You must constantly check the tension in your thread as you work," Edith said, leaning toward the young novice and correcting her stitches.

Isabelle was newly arrived at Wilton Abbey. Her mother had died and her father remarried. It had been decided shortly after that his daughter from his first marriage would be dedicated to the church.

Edith pitied the girl for being flung so far from home while still grieving for her mother. She speculated that it had been the stepmother who had sent her away. As homesick as she was now, Edith was sure she would prosper. It helped she was already fluent in French and English and knew some basic Latin. In time she would settle into the monastic life and even come to love her newfound life.

For now, Edith had taken the girl under her wing and was happy to spend time with her whenever she could.

The ringing of a bell permeated the silence.

Edith blinked. "My, how quickly time passes." She

looked out the window. The blue sky was tinted with streaks of pink and deep orange.

Isabelle looked like a deer, ready to leap away at the first sign of danger.

"It need not concern you. As a nun you are a bride of Christ and set above the rules of the secular world," Edith said, turning back to her. The girl was the daughter of a Saxon lord, even though her mother had been Norman.

The tolling bell was the signal of the start of curfew. Since the time of William the Conqueror, all Saxons were to put out fires and return to their homes; otherwise they could face harsh punishments. It was a way to deter them from gathering and plotting fresh rebellion. Edith found it amusing that the usurper had feared being usurped. She couldn't comprehend why, even after all these years, the Norman kings still feared and treated their Saxon subjects unfairly.

"Let's go to the kitchens and see if there's something for us to eat," Edith said, rubbing at her stiff fingers. "My fingers have lost their nimbleness with age."

Isabelle giggled. "You aren't old, my lady."

Edith grinned. "Perhaps I do not look it, but I'm over twenty now and should've long ago been wed either to a man or to God. Unfortunately, since no husband is forth-coming, I must wait. A pity that, unlike you, I am not given permission to take the veil. I am stuck at a crossroads and perhaps I shall be until death takes me."

Isabelle crossed herself. "Do not speak so. You never know where life might lead you but I shall pray for your continued health and well-being."

"Thank you, Isabelle. That is kind of you to include me

in your prayers." Edith glanced out the window at the sky again. The colors were stunning. She wished she could capture them in thread. Then, shaking out of her melancholy, she smoothed a hand over her bodice and adjusted her sleeves so they were no longer crinkled and tucked away.

In the two years since her brother had been anointed as King of Scotland, she'd been humbled. Her own pride had been tempered by the experience of losing her sister and finally acknowledging she couldn't have her own way. Even though she was certain she had done the right thing by scaring off her last two suitors she knew had a tendency to be selfish. Other suffered because of actions she had taken and she couldn't go on pretending that wasn't so.

Her antics of dressing like a nun were cast aside. Now she dressed as a proper princess should. Her long black hair was braided with ribbon into two long braids. Overtop this, she wore a simple white linen veil and a circlet to hold it in place. Her dress, gifted to her by her sister, was fashionable, a fitted bodice with wide sleeves and a pleated skirt. It was a crimson red, a vibrant color she would've abhorred in years past. But it reminded all who saw her of her Scottish and Saxon ancestry.

Her brother gifted her lands in Scotland and every year sent her the rents collected from them. Most of this she redistributed as alms to the poor. Despite her improved status, her troublesome reputation preceded her and no one else had asked for her hand in marriage.

There was also trouble in the kingdom. Rober, Duke of Normandy had returned from the Crusades and there were rumors he was launching an invasion on England. Edith doubted the king had little time for matchmaking while he worried about defending his kingdom.

There was unrest across the country, from angry peasants to rebellious nobles. For once, Edith was grateful to not be a key player in the power struggles.

Arm in arm with Isabelle, they made their way through the inner courtyard toward the kitchens.

It was then she heard a commotion by the gates that had her stopping in her tracks. The sounds of a woman screaming made her jump in fright.

"What is that?" Isabelle asked.

"I don't know. But I believe I must go see and intervene if possible," Edith said. "You should go on ahead."

"I won't leave your side," Isabelle said, even though she was clearly frightened.

They ran toward the sound coming from the front of the church.

Edith stepped out the gates to find a group of guards harassing a bedraggled woman, who was holding on to an infant. When one of the guards put his hand on the hilt of his sword, Edith cried out.

"What is going on here?" she asked with all the authority she could muster.

The men drew back and turned to face her. The hard look in their eyes melted away once they recognized her.

"Princess, this wretch was caught wandering the streets. She's Saxon, she knows it's against the law," the leader of the guard said, spitting on the ground as if he tasted something foul.

"She was on her way to church. That's hardly what I would call wandering the streets."

"The law—" The guard began speaking, but Edith interrupted him.

"She must have a good reason for breaking the curfew. Madam," Edith said, turning a kind smile to the bereft woman, "what reason do you have for traveling after curfew to the church doors?"

The woman looked helpless, and Edith realized she didn't speak French. The guards likely had not realized this either. She repeated her words in English this time.

The woman cried out in relief and said, "My son is ill. He has a fever and I feared for his life. I needed to come pray for God's intercession. I knew it was against the king's law, but I had to save my boy. My only boy." She revealed the small boy in her arms. His eyes were closed, but he was moving about fretfully.

Isabelle put a hand to her mouth. "*Sacré bleu.*"

Edith rounded on the guards with fury in her eyes. "It is your duty to protect this abbey and uphold the king's law. However, the law was put in place to prevent rebels from meeting and plotting treason. How does this poor woman fall into that category? You were bored and eager to make sport of tormenting her. The abbey keeps its doors open to all who need help. Whether they are Saxon or Norman. Return to your posts. I will help this woman since you cannot find it in your hearts to do so. Rest assured I shall ensure the sheriff is informed about this."

The men blanched and stepped aside.

Edith took the woman's elbow and led her inside.

The prioress was standing in the shadows of the entrance. Edith stopped before her, bowing her head. "I hope I wasn't wrong to intercede on this woman's behalf. You can see her need is dire."

The prioress was a hard woman, but her heart wasn't made of stone. "I commend you for your bravery." Turning to the woman, she asked her for her name.

"Eadburh, Sister," she said in English. "This is my son, Wulfrun. My husband, Leofric, is a blacksmith in the village. I didn't know where else to go." She sobbed. "The local wise woman could do nothing for him."

The prioress put her hand on the sleeping boy's head. "He is burning up with fever. We shall take him to our infirmary. Perhaps we can help him."

Eadburh kneeled before her and kissed the hem of her robe. "Thank you, thank you, I am grateful to you."

"Be grateful to God, for it was his intervention that brought Princess Edith to your rescue."

Eadburh nodded.

The prioress glanced at Edith and said in French, "You may go about your business. I shall look after her from here on out."

Edith nodded but before the prioress could turn away said, "And any expenses she incurs I will pay from my own purse." Turning to the confused woman, she said in English, "You needn't worry about anything other than your son's wellbeing. I am sorry you have had to suffer."

Once they were out of sight, Isabelle wiped at the corners of her eyes. "Will the boy survive?"

"His mother has given him the best chance by risking her life to come here. Those guards would have thrown her into prison or far worse. Her husband was a coward for not coming with her."

"Perhaps he was more scared of breaking curfew," Isabelle said.

Edith smiled at the young girl. She had so much to learn about the world, but she tilted her head. "Perhaps you are right. You may go, Isabelle. Tomorrow you will face a full day of work and study."

"But what will you do?"

"I will do as I said. I will go to the chapel, kneel before the Blessed Virgin and pray for her intercession."

Fifteen

It was well past midnight, the sky outside was pitch black, and Edith was still on her knees praying fervently when a hand touched her shoulder.

She let out a gasp and, turning her head, she was greeted by the sight of a ghost. She blinked and saw that no, indeed, he was here in front of her.

"Brother Turgot! What are you doing here?" she asked incredulously.

"The same might be asked of you, Princess Edith."

"I—I am praying on behalf of a mother and her sick son. It is the least I can do since I have no skill or knowledge of medicine."

He inclined his head. "That is honorable indeed. But you must take care of your own health."

Castigated, Edith nodded. Crossing herself, she got to her feet and found her legs were numb from the time she had spent kneeling.

"Steady, my dear lady," Turgot said, offering her his hand.

She took it and was certain at last he was not some apparition.

He had aged. His hair was now fully gray and time had etched deeper lines into his face. Yet for all that, she could feel his strength as he supported her while she walked to the bench.

"You are surprised to see me, no doubt," he said. "Your brother has sent me to England to be his representative at King William Rufus's court. He also entrusted me to look after both his sisters."

Edith looked down at her lap. "Mary is no longer at the abbey, as I'm sure you've heard. I'm afraid it was my doing as punishment for my defiance."

He tilted his head and regarded her sympathetically. "You've been ripped away from everything you know. Yet I am glad to see you have not fallen into despair. Perhaps in the end it was for the best that your sister left your side. I have seen her with my own eyes and she is thriving under the care of Lady Phillipa. She has sent gifts for you." He pulled out a small parcel from his pocket.

Edith didn't hesitate to open it. Inside she found a beautiful blue silk scarf. Birds in flight were embroidered on it with silver thread that caught the candlelight of the church. She marveled at her sister's talent, touching the embroidery reverently.

"It is beautiful. I shall write to thank her for it."

Turgot nodded. "I am sure she will appreciate it. She keeps you in her thoughts and was insistent that I tell you she misses you greatly and hopes you may find some way to see her again."

"I should like nothing more, but I am not allowed to leave Wilton Abbey."

"Things change. Soon enough you might find yourself married and free to come and go as you please."

Edith gave him a strained smile. "If God wills it, then I shall not deny him. But he has not called me to that holy state."

Turgot raised an eyebrow. "Rumors have reached Scotland that you have spurned your suitors. Men are terrified to think of approaching you now."

With a glint of mischief in her eye, Edith said, "Then they are cowards, not worthy of my hand."

Turgot laughed. "I see time has not dampened your spirit. Will you allow me to advise you as I once did your mother?"

Edith nodded.

"First, I shall defer all discussions of marriage for the time being. I want you to rest. Acting as if everything is within your power to fix and attributing all mishaps to yourself is the sin of pride. Think of how your mother failed to look after herself and perished prematurely."

"Of that I am guilty," Edith said. "But I shall do as you say and rest. Tomorrow will be a new day and I will need my strength if I am to help that woman and child."

Turgot nodded approvingly. "Your mother would be proud of the woman you have become."

The following day after she broke her fast, Edith visited the infirmary. The infant had survived the night. He was nearly a year old and still had the chubby cheeks of infancy.

A nun was dabbing his forehead with cool water while his mother slumbered, half draped over the bed and half on the floor.

Edith was carrying a bowl of hot porridge and a chunk of bread on a tray and set it down gently on a table nearby.

She inquired about the patient. "Will he live?"

"The worst is over," the nun whispered. "We've given him a concoction of bark, cloves, and honey to help him fight the infection. Near daybreak he awoke and took a few sips of broth before slipping back into sleep. Only after that did his mother sleep. I tried to reassure her, but I don't know English."

Edith crossed herself. "I am so grateful for your tender care, as I am sure she is as well. I shall translate for you whatever message you wish me to give."

The nun looked relieved. "Once he wakes, he should be kept in bed for at least two more days. He needs to keep taking the medicine to make sure the fever doesn't return. Then he will need to eat a hardy diet to strengthen him against further bouts of illness.

"I shall tell her," Edith said, already knowing that this woman couldn't afford such luxuries for her son. But she was determined to help and was already counting out the coins the woman might need.

The nun left the bedside to go tend to the other patients in the infirmary. Many came to Wilton Abbey for treatment. At the moment, a traveling merchant was resting in bed with a broken leg that the surgeon had set straight with a cast. Others lay about with various ailments. Edith took some time to fetch patients blankets and hot broth from the kitchen before returning to the sleeping woman and child.

She wondered if it would be wise to wake the mother. However, she needed to eat if she wished to maintain her strength to continue caring for her son. The porridge, still steaming on the table, was best when eaten warm and so Edith nudged her gently.

The mother started, her eyes wide as she blinked away her sleep.

"Fear not, Eadburh, all is well. I thought you might like something to eat," Edith said.

"My son?"

"The nun caring for him said his fever is breaking. Your little boy is strong and will recover, thanks to your bravery."

Eadburh crossed herself. "Thank you, my lady."

"Don't thank me. Thank God."

"I shall," she assured her and nodded her head.

"Come sit over there by the table and eat your fill."

Eadburh gripped her hand. "My lady, I have no money with which to repay you. My husband—truth be told, he has abandoned us. Fleeing three days ago with his tools."

Edith gasped. "Where has he gone?"

"To London, if I were to guess. It would be easy for him to find work there. He has ambitions to join a guild, even though I told him it was not such a straightforward thing to do."

"How could he abandon you and his child?" Edith was horrified.

The woman shrugged. "It happens often enough. I have carried many children in my womb, but this little boy is the only one to survive. When he fell ill, my husband said I was cursed and that he would not wait around to watch yet another of his children die. Perhaps he is right—"

"No," Edith said in uncontained rage. "He is a coward for abandoning you as he did. A true man would've stayed by your side and seen it through one way or another."

Eadburh let out a pained cry. "But regardless, my child and I will be cast out on the street next quarter day when I can no longer pay the rent. Without my husband, I am doomed."

Edith bit her bottom lip. Eadburh soothed a hand over her sleeping son's head.

"I will help you find work. The abbey always needs servants. It wouldn't be the freedom you are used to, but you'd have food and shelter. If your husband came back—"

"I wouldn't return to him," Eadburh said.

Edith pitied her because even as she said the words she hung her head, knowing she would have to be a dutiful wife and return to him.

"Eat. I will speak to the abbess and return momentarily."

"Bless you, my lady."

In the privacy of the corridor, Edith wiped away the hot angry tears that streamed down her face.

All her anger at the injustice of the world welled up inside her and she found she couldn't take it anymore. But crying wouldn't help anyone, so, wiping her eyes with the back of her sleeve, she went in search of the abbess.

Hawise was in the rectory, eating her morning meal. She looked unsurprised to discover Edith wished to speak to her.

"My child, sit at my side and eat something. You look pale."

"I am merely tired, Reverend Mother, but I wish to speak to you about more important matters. The woman who came seeking help for her son—"

"I have heard all about that," Hawise said, wiping her chin with a cloth. "You interfered and helped a poor woman in need."

"Yes. I hope I did not do something wrong."

Hawise's smile was soft and patient. "You've come to ask me if I can help them. Perhaps she needs money or a job, but I cannot give her or you what you are looking for."

"There is plenty of work in the abbey she could do."

"And plenty of people waiting in the rafters to do it." Hawise shook her head gently. "What I mean to say is there are many in need and wishing to come work at our abbey. I wish I could provide work for all the downtrodden. But I cannot help you with this."

Edith wanted to rail at the world all over again. But instead, she took a steadying breath and said, "If I were to take her on as a servant you would—"

Hawise shrugged. "I could not stop you. If you have the funds, that is. However, regardless of what you do, I want to remind you that you cannot help everyone in need. As hard as that may be to accept. Even if you had all the riches in the world."

Bowing her head, Edith nodded. "I do understand. I shall speak to the woman more. If I feel she can be of service, then I will take her on, and if not, then I shall try to find some other way to help her."

In the end, Eadburh made quite the case for herself.

"If my husband doesn't return within the year I will be free and I would wish to return to my family in Essex. They have a little farm and would take me in. Until then I will serve you faithfully. I am quick with a needle and I can cook and clean. You shall never have a reason to complain about me. My son will cause no trouble, I promise."

Edith nodded. "I think this sounds like an excellent proposition. Make any necessary arrangements and then you can start. I can afford to pay you for your room and board at the abbey as well as a shilling each quarter but no more."

Her expression was unreadable, but Eadburh curtsied and accepted. Perhaps the offer was disappointing but Edith would have to pay the monastery six pence a month for their food and board. All in all, she had acquired an expensive servant.

Bishop Osmund, passing through on his yearly visit to Wilton Abbey, asked to see Edith.

The saintly man had changed since the last time she had seen him. His eyes drooped and he walked with a pronounced limp.

"I'm growing too old to travel as I do, but my work is of far greater importance."

Edith crushed fresh strewing herbs into the fire, so he might enjoy the fragrant scent of lavender and thyme.

"The abbess tells me you've begun to help with the abbey's account books."

She nodded, pouring him some wine and adding a dash of nutmeg to the cup, just as he preferred it.

"And you've taken on a lot of extra work besides that," he said with a laugh as she brought him a stool for his feet.

"You needn't run about tending to an old man such as myself."

Edith grinned down at him. "It's only so you will tell me all the news. How is the king? Is there any news from Scotland?"

"The king is well, God willing. Perhaps soon he will take on a wife," the bishop said, eyeing her as he took a sip of his wine and smacked his lips. "You know you were mentioned as a prospective bride."

Edith shuddered. She'd never met him, but from the way he had taken her away her sister made her believe he was a vindictive man. It didn't help that he called the likes of Duke Alan and Earl William his friends.

"Rest assured, he refused to consider the idea." The bishop laughed at her shocked expression. "And now you are insulted."

"Pride is hard to put aside. Or so I am finding every day."

"Baw." He waved her away. "A bit of pride is good for a person. You temper it with your humility. Don't deny it. I see it in those little self-deprecating remarks. You fear letting your accomplishments go to your head. Many don't have the forbearance that you do."

"Like Prince Henry?" she teased.

"Funny you should mention him," he said. "The poor man's snuck off to Wales again."

"I can guess why," Edith said. It was an open secret that

Henry had taken a mistress in Wales. It was rumored she was a princess and a reported beauty. She didn't envy his freedom to find love where he pleased but disapproved of how he was wasting his time on frivolous pursuits. There was so much he could be doing with his time.

The bishop arched his brow, and Edith hurried to explain lest he think her jealous.

"He never found much happiness at his brother's court and he hates being a hanger-on. With no wars to fight he must feel aimless and would prefer to be far from people who are quick to insult him. It's a shame there's not more affection between the brothers."

"A great shame," the bishop said, sighing. "Indeed, I am on my way to Westminster to settle matters with Archbishop Anselm. Things have gone too far in that department. The king will exile him if this goes on." He closed his eyes and rubbed his temple with his free hand. "I fear I don't have the energy I once did."

Edith kneeled at his feet. "Is there something I can do? Perhaps ask a physician to make you something to ease your pain?"

"No. This is nothing. I am growing old and I am not surprised that I have aches and pains. None of these are as great as what Jesus Christ suffered for us."

She nodded and stood again, moving about the room, stirring the fire and adding another log onto the flame to ensure he wouldn't feel the chill in the air.

"Your brother is doing well in Scotland. By all accounts he is well liked. He will be a strong ruler and a loyal ally for England. I am glad to see your father's line prosper."

Edith tilted her head in gratitude. "I know you were one

of those who urged the king to help my brother. Thank you."

He waved her off. "Enough of all this gratitude. If only it were food, then I would feast upon it."

Edith laughed. "Don't fret, the abbess has ordered the kitchens to prepare you a grand feast."

"And a goose?"

"Certainly. You deserve nothing less. You are lucky you came before we started the Christmas fast."

There was a twinkle of amusement in his eyes. "Almost as though I arranged matters that way."

"Almost."

———

Before Christmas Eve the abbess called her to her side and showed her a letter.

"Bishop Osmund has died, taken suddenly in the night just three days ago."

"That can't be," Edith said, putting a hand to her heart. "May he rest in peace."

"Yes, he was a peacemaker in the realm. I wonder what will happen now that he is gone. He'd always been a fair man. Not the sort of man who could be bought or swayed by favors. When Archbishop Anselm was in the wrong, he wasn't afraid to tell him so. I fear the king didn't appreciate what a good advisor he was."

"He will be fondly remembered. The abbey at Sarum will stand as a testament to his work."

"And Archbishop Anselm? What will become of him? He's lost a friend and protector."

The abbess shrugged, less interested in this topic. "The last I heard, he is in Lyon. With the Pope at his back I suspect the king will eventually give into his demands. But I wonder if he will ever be welcomed back to England."

Edith nodded. "I shall retire to say a prayer for Bishop Osmund's soul. My prayers may count for little among all the others, but I would like to add my voice to them."

PART FIVE
1100

Sixteen

In the spring, Edith was surprised to receive a message from her uncle delivered by Prince Henry. He was riding through Wilton with a large party of friends. They were heading toward Sussex to celebrate Easter there and shore up support against the growing discontentment in that region.

She waited for him formally in the receiving room, with a maid and Eadburh to act as chaperones.

When Henry entered the room, he looked startled to find her sitting in a high-back chair. Sunlight flooded through the glass paned window behind her, must have stunned him.

She stood and curtsied to him as she ought to and waited for him to say something.

"Princess Edith, it's been far too long since I've last laid eyes on you."

She met his gaze straight on. "Almost two years, I believe."

"Has it really been so long? He scratched at the back of

his head, sheepish. "I had not meant to neglect you for so long."

"We've all been busy. I haven't had time to write my condolences to you regarding the death of Bishop Osmund. He is greatly missed."

Henry turned somber. "Yes. I was in shock when the news was first brought to me. I didn't want to believe it. My mother placed me under his tutelage when I was a young boy, and he's served me well ever since. My brothers like to tease me about my love of learning and called me a monk. In the past they hoped I would enter the church."

"But that is not your calling?" Edith wasn't sure why she asked such a personal question but was gratified he trusted her with a response.

"No. I suspect you feel the same. Dedicating my life to God would be an honor, but I feel he has greater purpose for me," he said. Then, with a lazy shrug, he added, "Or maybe I enjoy the comforts of this world too much to cast them aside for a holy life. I have learned that you never know where life will take you."

It was as if he had peered inside her soul. They were one and the same. When she finished pondering his words, Edith found he was scrutinizing her. Flushing, she returned to her seat.

"Will you sit? I've had a tray of sweetmeats and ale prepared for you."

He raised an eyebrow at her formality. "I'll take the ale. We still have ten miles to cover today if we are to reach our first stop in time."

"You are always on the road," Edith said, then motioned for her maid to bring him his drink.

"There are many benefits. Perhaps I do not have the comfort of a home, but neither am I bored or tied down to one place," he said, then stopped, fixing her with that impenetrable gaze of his. There was an unvoiced apology in his expression, for that was exactly what her life was.

"Life in a nunnery is far more interesting than you have been led to believe. There are wars over the best linen, and treasonous plots to claim the best room. I certainly don't have time to feel bored."

He grinned. "You shall have to tell me all your little secrets one day." He drank the ale in quick gulps. "I am glad you are enjoying yourself. Now when the king asks how you are faring I shall have a proper answer for him."

"And here I thought you came to see me because you missed my company."

"If that was so, I would never admit it. We are to be bitter enemies to the very last," he said.

Her smile was forlorn as she remembered her words after a particularly brutal game of chess where the both of them had been frustrated to no end. Bishop Osmund had insisted they end the game in a tie. She'd refused.

"That was many years ago. Time has softened my determination to dislike you."

"Has it?" he asked. Then, getting to his feet, he rolled his shoulders back. "But some things never seem to change. For all my prowess and loyalty I am still my brother's errand boy. He has granted me neither land nor money, so I continue to be beholden to him. Now I am off once again to try to quell some rebellion. If I am successful I shall receive nothing more beyond a pat on the head. Then he will allow his friends to go on debasing my name."

Edith stepped forward, placing a hand lightly on his forearm. "I thought you were fond of being called Deer-foot."

He scoffed.

"I would take it as a compliment. I recall the ancient Greeks worshipped the goddess Artemis, who hunted on foot, chasing after her quarry."

"So now I remind you of a woman?"

She laughed because she caught the spark of amusement in his eyes and knew he was teasing. "Let that be the last time I try to soothe you. You clearly don't need my sympathy."

He stepped back to bow to her with a dramatic flourish. Then brought her hands to his lips and placed a chaste kiss on one of her rings. "My lady, I pray you shall never change. Take care of yourself and continue fending off suitors."

"Why?"

He straightened, releasing her hand and putting on his leather gauntlets. "If I am to exist in this state of limbo, I must condemn you to do so as well."

Edith nudged his shoulder as if they were children at play. "Shall we bet on who can change their fate first?"

Henry grinned. "Yes, that sounds like an excellent idea. And what shall the prize be?"

His gaze dropped to her lips, but she could have imagined it. Not that she wanted to encourage flirtation. "That silver brooch of yours shall suffice, and I will offer you this armband in exchange." She held up her arm to show him the intricately woven gold band that encircled a polished lapis lazuli stone on her wrist. It was a replica of her mother's that she'd been forced to sell years ago.

"My lady, I believe what you offer is of far greater value."

She shrugged. "Perhaps I have more confidence in winning. Besides I do not wish to impoverish you by asking for something of equal value."

He put a hand to his chest, as though she had offended him greatly. "*Et tu?*"

"You are no Caesar."

"As I'm being constantly reminded," he said with good humor.

After he left, she found she missed his company, though she would never admit it to anyone else. That night she prayed for guidance. Edith wished to know where she belonged. Maybe it was time for her to marry or to ask to take the veil.

Edith slept fitfully. She'd spent the better part of the previous day in the scriptorium copying out manuscripts on thick vellum. The August heat had been oppressive and even a bath had not eased her suffering.

She longed for the cool autumn weather. She loved to watch the fields of golden wheat sway in the breeze.

Edith was lost in the pleasant memory when Eadburh stormed into her room. She sat upright, clutching her crucifix. "What has happened?"

"My lady, apologies for waking you," Eadburh said. At her side toddled the two-year-old Wulfrun. "But there's news from Westminster. Grave news."

Her dream-addled mind could only think of one thing. "Prince Henry?"

Eadburh gave her a knowing look but shook her head. "No, though this concerns him too. It's his majesty, King William Rufus. He has died."

Gasping, Edith clambered out of bed. "How?"

"A hunting accident, that is all I heard. The abbess is in the church. The priests will hold a special Mass for the king's soul."

"And wh-who will be the next king?"

Eadburh shook her head. "I don't know. I came immediately to tell you the moment I heard the news."

"May God rest his soul," Edith said and piously crossed herself. "I will dress and go speak to the abbess myself."

She was out of bed and hurried to select a gown from a peg on the wall. A simple black one would suffice. Behind a screen she threw it over her night shift and Eadburh helped her tie it. She didn't bother doing anything with her hair before hurrying out of her room.

In the church many elder members of the abbey had gathered. Abbess Hawise was unsurprised by Edith's sudden appearance and motioned for her to take a seat as she unfurled the official message from the court.

"As I was saying," she said, hating the interruption. "King William Rufus perished. A tragic accident befell him while he was out hunting in New Forest. At length his body was brought to Westminster and will be buried..."

Behind her Edith heard someone whisper, "It is the Lord's doing that he should perish in such a manner and place."

Edith tried to keep her expression neutral. Inwardly,

she couldn't help but agree with the nun's assertion. Over the years, the king had become a tyrant, imposing heavier taxes on the English people to fund his campaigns in France and his growing taste for luxury. While he entertained his friends with lavish banquets, his people were left to starve. Then, to make matters worse, he expanded the royal forests, banning any but those with his express permission from entering them. Several people were displaced from their homes to accommodate his desires. Many lost the ability to gather kindling and forage. Year by year, Edith had seen firsthand the number of beggars who came to beg at Wilton's gate grow.

"...Prince Henry, by grace of God, has inherited the kingdom. He will be anointed and crowned as soon as possible," Abbess Hawise said, setting aside the parchment. "We shall pray for the late king while we await further news."

Edith was frozen in her seat. Henry? King? And to think just a few weeks ago she'd called him a beggar. Her hand touched her wrist where the lapis lazuli band usually lay. She would have to send it to him. It was an insignificant thing compared to the far greater gifts he was about to receive.

The abbess dismissed them back to their beds.

Edith had no desire to sleep nor did she think her hammering heart would let her. What would this mean for her? Would Henry allow her to return to her brother's court in Scotland? Or would she remain here at Wilton?

Day by day more news reached the abbey, carried in by a breeze of whispers.

Sir Walter Tyrell had been left alone with the king while they were hunting. Some speculated that he'd been paid to assassinate the king. His friends had fled once it was clear the wound was fatal. No one wanted to be blamed. It was a shameful end.

Henry hadn't been near at hand, but upon hearing that his brother was dead, he wasted no time in taking control of the treasury and riding to Westminster to consolidate his position.

Bishop Osmund had taught him well. Henry didn't hesitate when the opportunity presented itself. Edith remembered their chess games and he'd often been relentless.

Two days later, a copy of the new king's coronation charter was brought to the abbey to be read in the town square for all to hear.

Edith was more interested in hearing about the coronation itself and questioned the messenger.

"I was lucky to be witness to it, my lady," he said, bowing his head. "It was organized quickly because King Henry felt there was no need to wait. Nor did he wish his people or the royal treasury to bear the expense of a grander coronation ceremony. Despite this, all was done as it ought to be. He was anointed by the Bishop of London, and all nobles who were in residence paid him homage. After this, there was great rejoicing among the people and celebrations in the city."

"I'm sure there was."

"He gave alms freely to those that had gathered and generously provided wine for all to enjoy."

She nodded. It was a good move if he hoped to gain the support and love of the people.

"Has there been any news from his brother, Duke Robert?"

"Not that I know of, my lady," the messenger said.

Edith nodded and gave him a penny for his troubles. "Thank you for your loyal service to the crown."

He smiled and went off in search of refreshment.

Edith studied the copy of the coronation charter.

Know that by the mercy of God and by the common counsel of the barons of England I have been crowned king of this realm. And because the kingdom has been oppressed by unjust exactions, being moved by reverence toward God and by the love I bear you all, I make free the Church of God...I abolish all the evil customs by which the kingdom of England has been unjustly oppressed.

She sucked in a breath as she read the words carefully. She could imagine Henry's sincerity as he dictated these words to the scribes, who eagerly copied down his words verbatim. Knowing him, he would've looked over every copy to ensure their accuracy before allowing them to be sent throughout the kingdom. His kingdom.

If she didn't have the charter in her hands, she would find it hard to believe. Under Henry's rule, England would have justice at last. Inheritances would pass from father to heir without bribes paid to the crown. Marriages could be arranged without the king standing in their way. And most shocking of all, he promised not to take land from the church following the death of an abbot or bishop. This had been a hotly contested issue between the clergy and King William Rufus.

Edith read on, noting with dry amusement, his reforms

included repealing the forest laws. The forest in which his brother had died would revert back to the people.

Of course, as often happened, the gossipmongers began to wonder if King Henry, tired of waiting for land and power of his own, had planned the assassination of his brother. He'd forgiven all murderers in his charter and that included Sir Walter Tyrell, who, once freed, fled for the continent.

Edith frowned at these rumors, believing in her heart they could not be true. Her fierce loyalty towards him surprised her.

SEVENTEEN

S lowly the excitement of August died down. Life had a way of moving on. There might be a new king, but that didn't stop time. Crops had to be harvested and animals cared for. There would always be cheese to be made, horseshoes to be hammered out, and swords sharpened against the coming days.

Edith walked with her maid, enjoying the scent of apples and pears ripening in the orchard when she heard a sharp call.

Alarmed, she turned toward the sound to see a page coming towards her at a run.

"What is it?" she shouted.

The man, gasping, said, "The king. The king has come!"

"What?" she gasped.

"His banners were spotted coming up the road. He's coming to Wilton."

Edith forced herself to be calm. He was probably just riding through or coming to enjoy the hunting in the deer park nearby.

"Princess, perhaps we ought to return to the abbey?" Eadburh suggested lightly.

"There is no need," Edith said primly. She wouldn't change her plans just because he was nearby.

"My lady, the abbess sent me to fetch you."

"What foolishness," Edith said under her breath. "Very well, we shall go back. Lead the way, sir."

The abbess studied her as she entered her private hall. "You certainly don't hurry when I summoned you."

Edith looked penitent. "I didn't think this was a matter of any urgency. If the king is riding through—"

With a scowl, the abbess shook her head. "Riding through? What nonsense. He's here for you."

Edith took a step back. "What do you mean?"

"Since the moment he was anointed the bishops have been pressuring him to marry. Many prospective brides were put forth, but he has made no reply. Now he rides to Wilton Abbey. It doesn't take a genius to figure out what this means."

Edith gaped. "No."

Abbess Hawise laughed. It was a cold, hard sound. "No? Is that what you will say when he asks you to marry him? Ha. You'd be a fool to do so. Well, at the very least, it will be interesting to see how he takes your refusal." She cocked her head to the side. "I thought you were partial to him. You've dined with him and met with him many times in the last seven years. You should be honored."

Edith gathered herself. "We are all jumping to conclusions. We cannot even be sure he is coming to visit me. Nor if he will broach the subject of marriage. It's all too ridiculous. We argue just as often as we laugh together. If he is coming to see me, it's because he feels a responsibility toward me, nothing more."

"We shall see, Princess Edith," Abbess Hawise said, inviting her to sit on a cushioned chair.

Anticipation building, Edith found it hard to sit still. She wrung her fingers in her lap while her gaze danced around the room.

Then a knock at the door snapped her out of her brooding and she shot to her feet. Abbess Hawise's eyebrow arched as she stood, arranging herself before she called out, "Enter."

The wooden door was opened by a herald, who announced in a loud proud voice, "King Henry." Then, bowing, he stepped aside to let the man himself enter.

As Henry stepped through the doorway, the room seemed to shrink. Both the abbess and Edith sank into deep curtsies. The other ladies with them followed suit. They stood like that with their heads bowed in deference until he bid them rise.

Edith's eyes immediately flew to his as though she would see past those dark eyes of his and straight to his mind. Why had he come?

A coy smile danced upon his lips as he took her in.

"Reverend Mother, I wished to travel to Wilton to thank you for all your hospitality in the past. I am now at liberty to repay you for all your kindness. Name anything you want and, if it is within my power, I shall grant it to you."

His courtly speech made the abbess smile and bob into another curtsy. Edith was sure she had a list of demands at the ready. It was politic to ask a newly minted monarch for favors in the early days, when he was bound to be carefree and generous.

Then Henry turned to her. "The last time I left I promised I would visit you more often, and so you see I have kept my word," he said, hands outstretched as if to prove he was there in the flesh. He was wearing a new mantle of silk that reflected the sunlight drifting in. His hair was oiled and, for once, his face was clean-shaven. If there was any indication his fortunes had changed, it was this.

"You honor me," Edith said, her gaze slipping from his. Then she stepped forward. "As per our bargain, I must give you this." She slipped the armband from her wrist and held it out to him. "We swore to compete on whose fortune would change first, and you've proven yourself to be the victor. Congratulations, Your Grace."

He hesitated a moment before encircling his hand around both the armband and her fingers. "May we speak?" He murmured the question.

"Certainly," she said primly. "You are the king."

A flash of amusement crossed his features. "So I am told. May we have a moment of privacy?"

Fearing Edith would offer some protest, the abbess spoke out. "The sun has not yet set. Why don't we sit out in the courtyard and enjoy the fresh air?"

"An excellent idea," Henry said, clapping his hands together. He offered Edith his hand and gingerly she placed hers in his.

"You are as flighty as a frightened cat," he commented. "I have never seen you act like this in my company."

"Before you weren't king and I wasn't at your command," she said. Her expression challenged him to correct her. He did not, but his eyes softened and he led her to a bench.

The others hung back but were still within sight. No one could accuse them of anything untoward. Yet by tomorrow Edith guessed the false rumors would spread across the country.

"Princess Edith, though I am a king now I would like you to answer me honestly. You never have to fear any retribution or punishment from me."

He looked at her so intently there was no mistaking his intentions any longer. She looked away, her cheeks burning. It was as though her greatest dreams and fears had rolled up into one.

"Your Grace, you must know my feelings towards marriage," she said, finding it difficult to speak.

He nodded, the gold chain he wore about his neck clinking with the movement.

"So please don't ask me," she whispered.

"Why?" His eyes snapped to hers.

"Because I might say yes—"

"And you don't want to?"

She looked away, but he drew her back to him like a moth to a flame.

"I've never known you to be afraid of anything, Princess Edith."

"I have nothing," she said, rushing to explain her reasoning. "You could make a far greater match than me. Perhaps to a French princess who will bring you lands. I am head-strong, overly pious, and I am not beautiful. I would make you a terrible queen."

"If you wish me to wax poetic about your beauty, I

shall," Henry murmured softly. His hand lifted as though he wished to reach out to stroke her cheek.

"Perhaps you are not the greatest beauty in the land," he conceded. A smile tugged at his lips when he noticed her glare. "Ah. See, my teasing has wounded you. You know your worth. For what it matters, I think you are quite beautiful. However, that is not what has captured my heart."

She had a hard time maintaining eye contact, but now, sensing he'd grown serious, she turned to regard him more closely.

His expression was sincere as he spoke. "England needs a queen. A good one to unite both Saxon and Norman alike. You've proven yourself to be intelligent, diligent, and astute. I could trust you to help me govern. As for your faults, what king would complain about having a pious wife?"

He winked. Edith forgot herself and laughed.

"Let me speak to you more practically since you won't be swayed by poetry. My kingdom is made up of two people. We've been divided, and old resentments left to ingrain themselves into the very fabric of our being. I have great hopes of expanding this kingdom, but we cannot if prejudices plague us. We must become one people. Through your mother you are related to Edmund Ironside. The blood of Saxon kings flows in your veins. I am the son of William the Conqueror, a Norman king. With our marriage we can begin the process of uniting this kingdom. Our children, should God bless us, would be both Saxon and Norman. They would put an end to the discord forever."

Edith felt the stirring of ambition at this great undertaking. She longed to jump at this chance, but she tempered her excitement with reality. He wasn't some besotted knight in a chivalric tale, moving mountains to be with her. Her heart was ready to look past all her misgivings, but she refused to allow her feelings to rule her.

"You have countless children born to you by diverse mothers." She tried to temper the stirrings of longing with the knowledge she wasn't the first woman he'd loved, nor might she be the last. Could she accept this? A small part of her wished he would deny the rumors.

"I will not lie and claim to have been abstinent."

She scoffed at the irony of his words. Any wife of his would be expected to come to his bed with her virtue intact. "I knew as much. It's common knowledge that men are often tempted by baser desires."

He chuckled but refrained from arguing.

"The succession would always be at risk. Those children would be older than any I bore you. Perhaps they'd try to claim the throne once you are gone or you might ask the Pope to legitimize them."

He shook his head. "They would be of no threat to our offspring."

Her lips pursed. There was more she wished to say but couldn't bring herself to. For one thing, she needed someone who would be constant to her. Would he marry her only to regret his decision and discard her? Would he flaunt his mistresses in front of her?

"There are many who have a claim to the crown of England. It would be impossible to pretend this wasn't the case," Henry said, speaking in soft tones. "I would safeguard our kingdom so that our children could safely inherit. But there is no guarantee. There never is."

"I know that," she said, bristling not at him but at the momentous decision she would have to make. There were so many unknowns. She both hated and loved him. Closing her eyes, she prayed for wisdom but found no answer.

"I can't give you a response," she muttered at last.

He let out a breath. "I will give you time to consider what I've said. I won't ask you yet to be my bride, but, even if I wished to, I cannot wait forever."

"I know that," she snapped. Then burst out laughing. "Even now we are arguing. How are we to survive being married to one another?"

"Well, it shall certainly make life more interesting, wouldn't you say?" He smiled a devilish grin. "I shall take my leave and pretend you have broken my heart."

"You mean to tell me I haven't? Perhaps you don't care for me as much as you should." She glanced up at him to find a smile dancing across his expression, his back hid her from all the watching courtiers and nuns.

He held out his hand to her and as he drew her up, whispered, "We are two sides of the same coin. I wouldn't love you quite so much if you didn't drive such a hard bargain."

With his bulk still hiding her from view, he placed a tender kiss on her palm that sent heat coursing through her. Flabbergasted, she remained frozen in place.

Then with a bow he departed without another word.

The abbess approached her. "So?"

"We spoke. There was no marriage proposal."

"What?" she half shouted out of incredulity. "What were you discussing then?"

Edith straightened her shoulders. "Marriage."

"Then—"

"We agreed that this was a serious matter that required proper consideration. He didn't ask me and I gave no answer. His Grace agreed to give me time."

The abbess clicked her tongue on the roof of her mouth in irritation. Raising her head up to the heavens, she said, "God, grant me patience."

A week later, her desire for time to contemplate her decision was often interrupted by letters and pressure from all quarters. Her brother, having been forewarned about the king's intentions, wrote to her urging her not to be a fool and to accept Henry's proposal. Even Turgot had visited her and in the same manner urged her to stop postponing. It was pointless to point out he hadn't actually asked her.

This pressure also had the added misfortune of making Edith want to dig in her heels. She fought her stubborn inclination that shouted for her to say no just to prove to them that no one commanded her.

Feeling lost, she turned to the one solace left to her: prayer.

The setting sun cast golden light in the chapel as she knelt. In the quiet, peace descended upon her at last and a powerful sense of certainty filled her.

Hearing footsteps in the church, she finished her prayer and rose from the floor.

Edith had expected to find the priest or some servant in the church, but instead it was Henry. She was startled by the unexpected sight. After remembering herself, she curt-sied to him.

His smile was warm as he regarded her.

"My lady, you will be sorry to learn the King of England has not slept a wink since the last time he spoke to you."

She didn't look sorry at all and he grinned at that. They had approached each other without realizing that they had done so.

"I am restless and cannot contain my impatience to have this matter settled once and for all." He bridged the gap between them, taking her hands in his, their fingers entwining as he asked, "Edith, Princess of Scotland, will you marry me?"

Her stubbornness and fear melted away then and she heard herself answering, "I will."

A blaze of happiness spread through him and he grinned in a most ignoble fashion. "You honor me."

"As you honor me," she replied, finding that joy had welled up within her too.

"Do you swear you wish to be my wife?" he asked, doubt entering his mind. "No one has coerced you?"

His hands squeezed hers lightly. She felt the strength of his arm and knew he'd defend England to his dying day.

"There were at least a dozen letters and lectures from my friends and family cajoling me to accept you. But I've come to the decision on my own. Perhaps against my own better judgment." Even now she couldn't help but tease him.

He let out an exasperated sigh. "I shall love you all my days." In a solemn oath, Henry placed a gentle kiss on the tips of her fingers even though they weren't alone.

She hushed him. "Don't make empty promises, Henry."

"I never do."

After Henry announced his intention to marry her, his political rivals objected. They thought she was an unsuitable choice and claimed she was a nun.

Despite Henry's horrified denials and her own, rumors spread across the country, leading to widespread disgust and outrage. The only way to resolve this was for a formal tribunal of bishops to investigate the case and prove beyond down there was no impediment to the marriage.

While she waited for the trial to begin, Edith was forced to watch as both their reputations were blackened by ugly rumors. Some claimed he had kidnapped her, while others accused her of being some common harlot. Her only solace at this time was her reunion with her sister.

Mary willingly left the comfort of the Countess' palace and returned to Wilton. Now they could walk among the herb gardens and the orchards, as they used to when they were children.

"And so you shall be a queen? I can't believe it," Mary said with a chuckle.

"I'm beginning to doubt it will ever happen. I cannot help but worry that our enemies will prevail."

Mary squeezed her hand. "You know what you need?"

"What?"

"A little faith."

Edith burst out laughing. As she wiped the corner of

her eyes, she said, "Oh, how I've missed you. I don't know if I can bear to be parted with you again."

"You make it sound like you will be," Mary said.

Edith smiled inwardly. She already had Henry's promise that he would find her sister a good husband. It had always been Mary's wish to be a great lady of the realm and soon she would be.

When Edith had worn a nun's habit as a disguise, she couldn't have predicted the trouble it would cause. Many witnesses, including her old suitor, William Warren, were called before Archbishop Anselm to give their testimony under oath.

Finally, it was her turn to be questioned relentlessly by the Archbishop and his peers.

"We have witnesses that even as a child at Romsey you wore a nun's veil. Your piety is well-known and you were often heard saying how you longed for the peace of spiritual life. Many believe you have already dedicated yourself to God. Do you deny this?"

Edith fought the inclination to look away from their disapproving expressions. Henry had invited Archbishop Anselm back to England so he could sit in judgement on her case. However, this had not softened the Archbishop to her. Thus far, he had been ruthless in his questioning.

Taking a steadying breath, she said, "I do deny it. It is true I am a pious woman but I know in my heart that I am not meant for the church. As many who knew me at Romsey will attest, I rejected the idea of becoming a nun with fervor. Even when my aunt pressed me to take the veil. There were many times when I was forced by circumstance to disguise myself as a nun but I swear on my immortal soul that I have never said any vows. I am not a nun and thus, am free to marry."

"That is for us to determine, Princess Edith," Archbishop Anselm said, his tone brisk.

Edith's gaze flicked to Henry, sitting on his throne nearby. He gripped the armrest in growing frustration. When their eyes met, he visibly softened, as though the very sight of her was enough to make him relax.

"Shall we proceed?" Another bishop asked with a cough.

Edith, confident that the truth would prevail, nodded.

Silence descended upon the congregation as Edith was anointed with holy oil. A bishop carried forth a beautiful ring made of gold. Her heart hammered as she noted the lapis lazuli stone in the center encircled by rubies and she knew that Henry had commissioned this especially for her.

Just three days ago they had wed. The sweet solemnity of the occasion still filled her with awe.

It had taken two months of preparations, not least because she had to wait for the bishops to deliberate on whether or not she was a nun. Even now, after Archbishop Anselm had declared she was free to marry, vicious rumors still circulated about her husband.

They alleged that after Henry had assassinated his

brother to seize the throne, he had also kidnapped a nun from a convent and married her.

Henry had been furious when he discovered that all his efforts had been wasted.

"I should've married you without putting you through that trial."

Edith hushed him, and ran her fingers through his hair until he had stilled and his mind turned to other, pleasanter things.

A silence fell on the congregation as the archbishop placed the crown on her head. As the choir began to sing, she felt the weight of responsibility fall upon her. She swore to herself she would be a mother to all her people, especially the poor and downtrodden. Out of habit, she searched the crowd for her husband, even though she knew Henry awaited her return at the palace.

Today would be for her and her alone.

Her spirits soared and peace filled her.

This was where she was meant to be.

As she rose from her throne, resplendent in her coronation robes, she ceased to be Edith and embraced her new name: Matilda.

It was common for queen's to adopt a new name after their coronation. It felt right to shed her old identity as she left her life at the abbey behind. She chose a Norman name as a way to assure everyone she would treat Norman and Saxon alike, with equal love and fairness.

The members of the clergy, nobility, and gentry who had crowded into the church to see her wed now cheered as she was presented to them as their anointed queen.

They processed through the city with her riding on a

magnificent white mare, yet another gift from Henry. She handed out alms and waved to the crowds of onlookers.

Back at the palace, she found a moment's respite when she was led to a private room to rest and recover before the banquet would start.

Her ladies and her sister fussed over her, trying to get her to eat and bringing her watered-down wine to drink.

"You looked splendid, Your Grace," Mary said, sitting on a stool at her side. "And what an unusual ring."

Matilda smiled and held out her hand so her sister could examine it more closely. "I have an affinity with the stone."

Before Mary could reply, the door opened and the king entered, dressed in elegant robes of vibrant blue.

Her ladies all dropped into low curtsies.

"My lord husband," Matilda said, reaching out to him.

He strode forward and kissed her hand before kissing her cheeks, and then at last her lips.

"My queen," he murmured against her ear.

With a snap of his fingers, he dismissed her ladies. Matilda caught Mary's sheepish wink in her direction as she closed the chamber door.

"Henry, what will they say?" She laughed as he fed her a candied apricot.

"They will say '*my, how the king dotes on his wife*,'" he intoned in a high-pitched voice that had her laughing all over again.

"They will think—" Her words were silenced by his insistent kiss.

Pausing to catch his breath, he said, "We are busy doing what every newlywed couple does..."

Her eyes dared him to go on.

"Our duty," he said, his lips brushing against her cheek.

She pushed against him half-heartedly, before drawing closer to him. "There is so much business to attend to. France is testing our borders..."

"Don't talk of war to me, woman. Not now." He let out a frustrated groan.

"You're right," she conceded, happily enough and wrapped her arms around his neck. "There's time for that later. There are marriage alliances we should consider for your—"

Henry let out a frustrated groan. "Is this how it will be? Will I always have to fight to draw you away from business?"

She nodded, coyly meeting his eyes. "Always."

Hope and happiness burned within her so strongly she thought she might burst. She pulled him toward her and sealed her words with a kiss.

AUTHOR'S NOTE

Matilda of Scotland, as she was known in the records, was born Edith and changed her name upon her coronation. Her marriage to King Henry was a successful one, and he left her as regent while he was away administering to his other lands on the continent. She was an active queen, who exerted her influence and patronage. She remained pious all her life and was dedicated to helping the less fortunate. At the time of her marriage, a council of bishops had been called to look into the matter of whether or not she was a nun. It was concluded that though she'd worn a veil from time to time to spurn suitors or protect herself while traveling, she had never taken vows. Yet even after her death the rumors persisted.

In an age when even many kings were illiterate, Matilda had learned to read and write in at least two languages. Her relationship with Turgot remained strong even after her coronation. She commissioned him to write an account of her mother's life. Margaret of Wessex was canonized in 1250 and from then on was known as Saint Margaret of

Scotland. Her brother Edgar died without issue, leading to her brother Alexander inheriting it. After him, her youngest brother David was crowned King of Scotland.

Her sister, Mary, got her wish and was married to the Count of Boulogne shortly after her sister's coronation. He was a wealthy man and the two were said to be very happy together. She died in 1116, two years before Matilda.

When Matilda died unexpectedly in 1118, she was remembered fondly by all as Matilda bona regina or Matilda the Good Queen.

While she had two children with Henry, only her daughter (yet another Matilda) survived. This plunged England into a succession crisis and bloody civil wars followed as Empress Matilda tried to claim the throne for herself against the contender, Stephen of Blois, Henry's nephew. Stephen was married to Matilda of Boulogne, daughter of Matilda's sister Mary. In the end, Matilda's son Henry II claimed the English throne and ushered in a new dynasty. There wouldn't be another Queen of England until Mary I in 1556.

As always please note some historical facts were fabricated or altered in this story. For example, while some sources claim that Cristina died before Matilda's marriage, others say she was the one to instigate the rumors about her being a nun. Above all, I hope you've enjoyed this story.

Printed in Great Britain
by Amazon